THE THINGS WE BURY

-A Rural Noir-

BAD DOG PRESS

THE THINGS WE BURY
Copyright © 2020/2022 Philip LoPresti

Published by **Bad Dog Press**

Cover design by Philip LoPresti

Second Edition 2022

ISBN-13: 978-0-578-38814-4

ALSO BY PHILIP LOPRESTI

Where It Hurts And For How Long
Tried In Ruin
Those Born In Darkness Never Seek The Light

For everyone with an unfulfilled dream, a burning rage, a sadness that just won't quit, a lost love, a minor regret, a madness carved from a shaded past, a ghost that always follows—**THE THINGS WE BURY** is for you.

THE THINGS WE BURY

CHAPTER: 1

Most of the time I don't care about living. But sometimes, although not often, I wish to live long enough to see my enemies die. But what do you do when you yourself are your only enemy?

X X X

A flash from the barrel and a kick from the recoil turn the world upside down, and, for a few brief moments, I feel like God.

But it doesn't feel as good as you'd think.

Then again, why would it?

Theft, broken bones, threats, steering wheels. I've loaded guns and hotwired cars. I've fed men lies, intentionally putting them at a disadvantage in order to take what was needed or simply what was owed. These are some of the things I've done with my own hands. I'm not proud of it, but I've done them, nonetheless.

But death? Murder?

Never.

Not with my hands anyway. With my actions, maybe.

Does that count?

I suppose I always knew the job would catch up with me. And it has. More than ever now, and in more ways than one.

I rush across the parking lot—away from the apartment complex—gun in one hand, duffel bag slung over the opposite shoulder. I wipe the blood from my face—feel an aching in my teeth—and with one flick of the wrist, fling it from my palm to the pavement below. I swear I can hear it smack the asphalt and get caught in the ruts.

Is that what killing a man does? Do you lose your mind right away or does it happen slowly, over time? Or maybe I've been losing it since I was old enough to know better.

When I reach the '72 Chevy Nova parked across the street, I look back over my shoulder at the near-empty parking lot. Coupled with the fact that no lights seem to be on in any of the windows, I take it as a sign that there are no witnesses to identify me or the shit-bucket I'm driving, but it doesn't stop me from beating myself up for having not parked two blocks over, rather than right out in front of a place where a murder just occurred.

I get in the car and toss the snub-nosed revolver and duffel bag onto the passenger seat and bring the car to life with the turn of a screwdriver, the tailpipe coughing smoke into the night as I drive off.

Halfway down the road and the taste comes on strong, thick.

Heated metal.

Raw meat.

Blood.

I spit onto the passenger side floorboard several times to rid my palette of the taste, but it does nothing. I reach into the glove compartment, grab some fast-food napkins, and jam them in my mouth to soak up any of the remaining blood that may have pooled along the sides of my tongue and teeth, and I'm thinking, *This shit gets everywhere*.

It wasn't supposed to go down like this. It was supposed to be an easy job. Break in, retrieve the bag, slip out undetected. I was told the apartment would be empty—made sure I showed up exactly at the time I'd been instructed so I knew there would be no chance of running into trouble. And then suddenly, I'm rolling across a carpet with some guy waving a knife like a madman.

I know that rage all too well.

He'd hidden himself in the closet. Was he waiting for me, or did he duck in there when he heard me enter? Was he also there for the bag? I should have let him kill me. How the fuck did this happen?

I try to shake the image of half his head exploding off his shoulders in a burst of mulch and marinara paste, but it is quickly making friends with the other nightmares I have rolling around up there.

Maddie, the birds, and the starving baby.

I roll the window down and spit the tissue into the damp night and replace it with a cigarette. I fire it up, sucking back three quick drags to calm my nerves. The sting of cold air feels good on my face. I close my eyes and contemplate letting it turn my skin to sandpaper. I debate whether I should ever open my eyes again. It could be easy this way. Just keep driving. I'd never see it coming, just feel the impact swallow me whole. I think better of it. There are enough dead people on my hands. No need to add an entire family to the list.

It is thoughts like this that keep me going most of the time. Thoughts of suicide.

This is how I survive.

I open my eyes, toss the cigarette to the dark outside, and watch the embers scatter themselves along the road in the rearview mirror. Pangs of blood push at my temples. The road ahead cuts like a river through walls of strong maples and dying oaks. There are very few streetlights in places like this. As if someone thought the residents of low-income areas were better left in the dark, away from the eyes of the rest of the world. Tucked away like fucking lepers. As if this way of living is contagious.

Even in the dark, I catch glimpses of the financial ruin plaguing small areas such as this one. It is places like this that get hit first and hit the hardest in the face of economic collapse. Both sides of the road are littered with homes that are mere shells of what they used to be, many of them having been abandoned when residents could no longer keep up on mortgage payments or repairs due to loss of jobs. Others are burnt-out husks due to meth lab conversions followed by meth lab explosions, the windows blown out, and streaks of seared black running up toward the roofs. The few remaining lived-in homes—most of which are one strong wind away from becoming like the rest—have smoke billowing from the chimneys on this cold November night and I am left wishing that Maddie was still alive.

I light another cigarette and squint against the smoke that's reaching for my eyes. My rib cage itches from all the scabs forming and there's a dull ache where my head should be. I pull out the piece of paper I have tucked in the sun visor, cigarette dangling from my lips, and study the address written on it. I repeat it back to myself four times before deciding that changing the plan is the best course of action.

Corsetti won't be happy. He might even want to finish what the guy back there started, but the death of a man tends to change things.

I crush the paper in my fist and stuff it in my mouth, chewing it until it's nothing more than scraps of pulp clinging to my tongue. When I'm absolutely sure that's all that remains, I swallow the wet pieces, tasting ink as it goes down.

I need to keep driving. Find another place to lay low. I'm getting tired. I haven't slept well in months but feel like wings could burst from my back at any moment. I want to chew through my own wrists, to the other side of this insanity, and find some thought that could cure me of the disease that is myself, but I just gag and cough and stub the cigarette out on the dashboard instead.

X X X

I drive until I feel I've put enough miles between me and the mess I just caused, although to be fair, no number of miles are enough when the dead are on your hands. That kind of shit will chase you until you're lying right there next to them.

After what feels like a month-long bender spent inside my own head, I finally find a motel where I can lay low, make some phone calls, and figure out my next move. It's one of those pay-by-the-night joints tucked away from civilization. A one-floor stucco building with a dozen rooms or so—the sort of place where trash litters the surrounding property and clusters of plastic bag ghosts hang from the limbs of surrounding trees. I wonder what kind of business a dive like this gets in the first place. You'd have to know exactly where to find it. It's not exactly the kind of place you just stumble upon on your way through. And yet, here I am doing exactly that.

I pull into the parking lot and park the car and kill the engine. I leave the screwdriver jammed in the ignition, like I always do, but take the duffel bag and gun with me.

Outside, I lean against the front of the Chevy, tuck the gun in my waistband, and try to compose myself. I close my eyes, inhale deeply, and wait for a five-count before letting the air from my lungs. I open my eyes and I'm still in the same sinkhole I was before I closed them. I glance around the parking lot. There are no other cars. No one else here, hopefully. I don't need any more mishaps. It's cold and getting colder. I zip up my jacket and watch my breath swirl and dissipate before making my way to the entrance.

Once inside, I use the counter to support my weight, suddenly feeling heavy with the need to sleep. I ring the bell that sits in front of me. The sound reverberates through my head, and I close my eyes and clench my teeth to stave off the sound from traveling too far back into my skull, where a headache is still trying to form a tiny army.

From the backroom, I hear footsteps and the shuffling of papers. After a few moments, a man appearing to be in his twenties, but just as easily could be in his fifties limps out. His face shows signs of heavy drug use. Just one of the many casualties an area like this has to offer, I'm sure.

"What can I do ya fer?" He asks.

I can't tell if he's mocking the locals or if he actually talks like that.

"I need a room," I say, leaning on my elbows and taking in his features, which have become clearer now that he's standing right in front of me. It's worse than I thought. His face cuts at thin, uneven angles and is worse for wear. Scabs pepper his skin. His eyes are two black stones tossed to dirt and his teeth are a muted yellow, with gums letting go and crammed with chewing tobacco.

"Sure thing. It's thirty dollars a night, twenty-five if you're staying three nights or more and we only take cash. You can pay for the first night now and we'll work out the details tomorrow if you're staying longer."

Having already seen this place from the outside, I can't imagine anyone wanting to stay here more than a couple of hours let alone a few days, but I'm here for as long as I need to be. I agree to the terms and the kid slides a clipboard with a sign-in sheet attached to it toward me. I sign a name, dip into my pocket, and produce two twenty-dollar bills, handing them over to the young man who looks fifty.

"So, how long will ya be stayin' at the Mossy Oak," he eyes my signature, "Mister Blackwell?" He slides the room key across the counter.

"Your guess is as good as mine," I say. I palm the key and walk out, convinced this place is just a front for selling drugs.

CHAPTER: 2

The room is exactly what you would expect for thirty dollars a night. When I enter, I am immediately hit with a damp, musky aroma—a smell that tells me no one has stayed here for months, maybe even years.

I trace the interior of the room with my eyes. The wallpaper is peeling in areas, half an inch of dust covers everything, and the bedding looks as if it hasn't been washed, ever. Normally I wouldn't even entertain the idea of sleeping on these sheets. In my younger years, I would have turned right around and hauled ass back to the front desk to have words with motel management. Nowadays I seem to be doing a lot of things I wouldn't have normally done. Amazing what you let slip when you're almost pushing forty and your dead wife is haunting your every move. Besides, I just had a mouthful of a stranger's blood. Nothing I'm going to catch from these sheets I haven't already from gargling the blood of a man who I had known only seconds prior to taking half his head off.

I throw the duffel bag on the bed and stuff the gun under the mattress before walking to the TV that is sitting on a dresser opposite the bed. It's old. The kind with the rabbit ear antennas. I need some background noise to drown out some of my current situation and my ever-present thoughts that aim to end me.

I pull the knob and the screen stays black.

I notice a crack in the bottom right-hand corner, pieces of it have fallen away as if someone used it to bludgeon a lover to death. Probably did. This isn't the kind of place you'd stay on your honeymoon. It is better suited for murder brought on by jealousy and betrayal.

I reach around the back of the television and grab hold of the cord, reeling it in. It comes with no resistance. The end is a frayed mess with no prongs to plug into an outlet. Probably chewed away by one of the many animals that found its way in over the years—or maybe a former guest having gone mad at the first sight of this dump.

On the nightstand is a radio. I try it and to my surprise, static erupts from the speakers. I turn the dial until a station comes in clear, and I catch a voice welcoming late-night listeners and thanking people for donations which help keep the local station going. He says it's the best station for classic blues, country, and jazz. A song begins. A low twang fills the room and I recognize the song as a Hank Williams number, but the title escapes me, but from the sound quality, they still play vinyl.

I leave the radio playing and go into the bathroom. I stare into the mirror, hesitant to turn on the light. I know what can happen. I reach for the switch and see myself staring back—a hundred and seventy-pound sack of failed dreams. The lines on my face are becoming more defined, deeper. Grooves that hold too much hard truth. The patches of grey hair, like weeds now, invading what was once a healthy growth of thick brown hair. When did this happen? When does age begin to show itself? It doesn't seem like that long ago that my shoulders were broad with confidence. Now I am walking in my own corpse.

Breaking eye contact with myself, I notice the tub in the mirror's reflection—one of those old cast iron jobs with the claw feet. It's the cleanest thing in this place and I think, *Should I eat a bullet now or drown myself later?* I could baptize myself by doing so. Be reborn. Emerge lighter, cleaner, free of regret.

Sometimes, birth is the messiest part. Other times it's what follows which you can never wash clean.

I turn on the faucet and splash cold water on my face, hoping to stun the thoughts loose from my head. It does very little. They are holding on white knuckle tight. Where did it all go wrong?

In my mid-twenties, I had vowed to get sober, and I did. I stopped having meaningless sex and even started eating right. That was when I found Maddie. She was hunched in a doorway to keep out of the rain. We fell in love. Had amazing sex. Lived together. Had a child and got married, carrying one another off to heaven. But then I fell back into my old routine, the shadows of my past calling me back down familiar alleyways and I was too quick in answering the voices. Then Maddie was wrenched from me for something I no doubt did in a past life. That's what I tell myself on a good day anyway. Truth is, my aim has always been shit. My mistakes hit those who are closest to me when they should be maiming me instead.

I hate the person staring back at me, now more than ever.

I grow tired of looking at my face, so I punch the mirror and spend the next twenty minutes pulling glass from my knuckles.

I decide I want a bath.

The tub is too small. No matter what position I bend myself into, either my knees or my feet are exposed to the sting of cold air outside of the warm water. I decide to let my knees take the hit and lean back against the aged lining, music drifting in from where it still plays in the other room.

I stare down through the water at my naked self—at the scars. I run my fingers over the ruts on my stomach, ribs, and other places. One cut for each day she's been gone. I'm careful most of the time, but every so often I go too deep.

This is how I survive.

From the corner of my eye, I catch a glimpse of a shard of glass from the broken mirror lying on the floor. I lean out of the tub, stretching myself to the point where I can feel the scabs along my rib cage breaking open, and swipe it from the dirty tile. I hold it under the water and wave it around, attempting to sterilize it the best I can as if there's any point in doing so.

I run the jagged piece of mirror along my leg, and I can feel my skin split open. I butterfly the epidermis with two fingers as one might do to a labia and I half expect to see insects scatter from the opening and take to the water where I can watch them drown. But instead, I just watch blood push its way from the wound in a hypnotic rush of red before coming to rest at the top of the bathwater where it floats before turning a dull pink and getting lost to the suds.

I think of Naomi. I wonder what she's doing. If she's sleeping well. She is prone to nightmares too, something I no doubt passed down to her. I close my eyes and I can see her standing in the doorway of the bedroom Maddie and I shared, her nightgown just a bit too long, sweeping the floor with her movements. She holds her stuffed owl to her chest and asks us if she can sleep in our bed. Only eight years old and she is the spitting image of her mother but seems to harbor demons like her old man. What a thing to pass down to your child, then I think, *it's more than my father ever passed down to me*. I hope she doesn't spend the rest of her life running from her own thoughts. It's a battle no one ever wins.

I should call my parents' house and ask to speak to her. I can ask my mother how my father is doing too, but I won't. Not now anyway. The less she hears my voice, the more likely she is to forget me and get used to a life without my presence. It seems cruel for me to deny her a father, what with her mother being gone, but it's for the best. I am no good for anyone, least of all an eight-year-old girl who needs direction in her life, regardless of if she was cut from the same blood and bone as me.

I pull myself from the bath and dry off, after which I crazy glue the cut on my leg closed—something I do when I've gone too deep. I get dressed and pace the motel room carpet while taking swigs from a flask and smoking cigarettes.

And still the music floats.

I think of phoning Corsetti. I have to inform him of the body I left behind. No telling how he'll react, but

I know it's best to deliver the news myself and get it over with.

Sitting on the edge of the bed, I turn down the radio and balance the phone on my knee and dial out. It takes a few rings and then a voice I've never heard before answers.

"Yeah?"

"Hey, is Corsetti in?"

"Who's askin?"

"Tell him Fenton Marciano is on the phone."

"Hold on."

I've never actually met the man. All my dealings with him have been over the phone or through messages delivered to me by one of his goons. It had always been this way. After I met Maddie and she got pregnant with Naomi, I left the street life in pursuit of a family one, but in my younger years, I had done low-level jobs for Corsetti. That is until the bills started mounting and Maddie and I couldn't keep up. I know she didn't want me to return to this life, but I wasn't about to let my family go hungry or homeless and Corsetti offered me a way out.

There are some who don't believe the man even exists. As if he's some sort of boogeyman of the criminal underworld. Even the police didn't buy the idea of him being any one person, but more of a collective of local criminals operating under one name. He seemed to control too much turf for it to be just one guy. Regardless of whether that was true or not, I always spoke to the same man.

"Fenton?"

"It's me."

"Did you get what I asked for?"

"I did, but there was a bit of a mishap." There's hesitation in my voice and he knows it.

"Oh yeah, and what is that?" His voice is suspicious now. I can tell that he's prepared to give the word and have two mooks out here in no time to snuff me out.

"I, uh, I sort of killed someone."

"Tell me what happened." His voice is calm now—almost soothing to hear—as if taking the life of another is no big deal or bears no consequence on one's conscience.

"I entered the residence to retrieve the bag and the fucker was waiting in the closet. Took me by surprise. We rumbled, he lost."

"And you're sure he's dead?"

"I sure fuckin' hope so because he's gonna have a hell of a time gettin' around without his head."

"Any idea who it might have been?"

"Ahhh, shit, I forgot to check his ID."

"You fuckin' wise-ass."

"Well, how the hell am I supposed to know who he was? Like I said, he was waiting in the closet. I don't know if he was there for the bag, or just some tweeker looking to score some shit to pawn. Either way, he's dead."

The deafening silence that follows causes me to start sweating, and my chest feels like it's going to cave in.

I break the dead air. "Listen, it wasn't supposed to be this way..."

He cuts me off. "Let me ask you a question."

"Okay."

"Why'd you bring the gun?"

He takes sips of something and waits for my response. I can hear ice clicking off his teeth.

"No?" He asks, following my silence. "No answer? I'll tell ya why then. Because you knew there was risk involved and because of these possible risks you weighed your options, which led you to a conclusion and your final answer was a gun. And lucky for you, you're a fuckin' genius or else it would be you without a head and not some other schmuck. There are no easy jobs in this line of work. There are no guarantees."

Truth was, I always carried a gun. I figured that if I had to pull it out in any given situation, just the sight of it would keep people on their best behavior. That was what I hoped anyway. I'd never planned to use it, despite going to the shooting range a couple of times a week to keep from getting rusty. Guess I'm just naïve in that way.

"Tell me what I do now," I say to him.

"Well, if this asshole is dead like you say he is, the cops will be all over it, so just sit tight and I'll send Jimmy and Sal your way to retrieve the bag and get you out of there. You at the address I gave you?"

"Well, not exactly."

"What do you mean not exactly? You either are or you aren't, so which is it?"

"I'm not."

I clam up, feeling words stuck in my throat. I don't know if I should apologize or end it all right now and tell him to go fuck himself. He'll have someone put the hurt to me bad enough. I'll have to be hospitalized, but it's not far off from what I want anyway.

Corsetti's voice comes through the line like rolling thunder.

"Are ya gonna fuckin' tell me where you are or am I gonna have these two assholes driving around the backwoods of bum fuck nowhere looking for your ass?"

"I'm about three towns away. Right outside a little place called Cedars Parish at some seedy motel called The Mossy Oak."

"Address?" He says it like he's talking to a child who doesn't know any better.

I give him the address and I can hear him scribbling on a piece of paper and then snap his fingers.

"Stay there. They're coming for the bag. Should be three days. Four tops."

"Three days? Listen, can't I just leave the bag somewhere, call back with its location, and get the fuck out of this Godforsaken place? The longer I stay here, the more I'm putting myself at risk. This whole thing has turned into a shit show."

Corsetti lets out a laugh, but underneath it, I can hear anger bubbling. "You know better than to ask a question like that. You've worked for me on and off for some years now, Fenton. I like you. You've never been a problem and coupled with what you've been going through, I'm giving you the benefit of the doubt on this one. I'm sympathetic to your situation. You know one of my own lays on his deathbed… "

He's referring to his son. From what little I've heard; he was born with a genetic disorder and time is catching up with him. He's in need of an organ, but donors are in short supply these days and, even still, he's not high enough on the list.

Corsetti continues, "I'm excusing the last-minute changes you've decided to make without my consent, given these circumstances, so stay put with the fuckin' bag and someone is coming directly to you. No funny business or I won't be as forgiving as I'm being now, capisce?"

"I understand."

"Good. Three days. Don't fuck this up."

The line goes dead.

I hang up the phone and place it back on the bedside table. I light a cigarette, take a deep drag, and turn the radio up loud. I close my eyes and pinch the bridge of my nose, the headache still trying its hardest to finish me off.

CHAPTER: 3

I toss and turn, my sweat soaking the mattress down to its springs. Fuzz, like television static, buzzes in my brain and I have ghosts in my blood. They are ever-present, always riding the flow. I never wanted this, but I only have myself to blame. After all, we are all products of the choices we make.

I push myself from sleep and meet the dark in a fit of thrashing and grabbing at the sheets. Ever since I was a child I've been plagued by nightmares. One involves me tracking and killing a magnificent bird. The terrain is always different, as are the tools I use to blast it from the sky, but the outcome is always the same. First, I always succeed. And second, as it lays there with its wingspan bloodied and flapping, I stand over it and look into its eyes feeling no remorse. Instead, I feel an overwhelming sense of anger. I then pick up a nearby rock and sunder the bird to a bloody pulp. In the end, my arms are heavy and all that remains are the stains, bones turned to dust, and bits of feathers caught in a cross-breeze which shudders me awake and fills me with dread.

Waking to face the dark only makes it worse.

These days I'm mostly haunted by Maddie and what she never told me. This thought seems closer now more than ever. As if it's corralling the rest into a small corner of my brain and making a home of all that space where it lives like cancer, slowly eating away at the better part of who I am. There isn't much left now.

Although maybe there was never much to begin with.

Toward the end, Maddie had nightmares of her own. What they were about, she never told me, but I remember some nights feeling her hand on my chest as she reached out through her dreams in what I think was an attempt to make sure I was still close. Now here I am, clawing my way through my own with no one on the other side to meet me. Although I must admit that some nights upon waking, I can hear my own voice speaking to her. I address the ether as if I'm writing a letter.

Dear Maddie,

It's been nine months, seventeen days, and twenty-two hours since you've been gone. I still get the urge. The one I get when looking in the bathroom mirror, but it's different this time. It comes on stronger and more frequently. I think it's because your reflection isn't there behind me anymore to pull me back from the ledge. It's funny, we seemed to have found each other at the right time, as if we were both waiting on the other side of our respective landslides to lick each other's wounds clean like a pair of wounded dogs, no matter the cost. You don't think about shit like that in the beginning. The price you might have to pay. The debt you may have hanging over your head for all time. You're too busy reveling in the idea that someone shares the same terrible sadness as you and you're eager to lose yourself in that truth, if you can call that a truth, and that's exactly what we did.

Loving you through that sadness was never the hard part though. That was one of the easiest things I've ever had to do. But possibly losing you because of it…that is the burden that at times, seems entirely way too heavy to carry. A burden I no longer want to lift, but one I cannot let go of either…

I lay in bed with all this close to the surface of me, slick and wet like oil spilled across a lake. I sit up and bite my bottom lip. The blood comes in a steady stream. I think I'm awake this time, but I can't be sure. I wipe the trickle from my chin and think, *If it weren't for these fuckin' nightmares, I could just sleep myself to death.*

I slink from the ratty mattress and dig through my jacket pockets for the bottle of aspirin. I pop a few and chew them to powder, after which I wash it down with a drink of water straight from the bathroom faucet.

If you wait too long to swallow, it all turns to paste.

The cuts on my knuckles have opened again. I tear a strip from the bedsheet and wrap my hand, watching the blood bloom through in fractured inkblots. I decide that sleep isn't an option, so I throw on some clothes and leave the room.

Outside, I light a cigarette. The air is frigid and damp. I can feel it in my lungs—my bones. Late fall in Upstate New York is an ugly site. The trees, which were full of beautiful shades of red and orange just weeks prior, now stand empty and naked, lonely in their structure. The surrounding fields, on the verge of being blanketed with a light snowfall, lay bare, the grass and strawroot now turned a muddy brown, nature having quelled its progress. I hate snow but am always eager for the first snowfall to cover up the eyesore that stretches to the hills and beyond.

Maddie loved snow.

Every time I had to shovel the stuff after a heavy snowfall I'd mumble and curse under my breath and she would just smile and shake her head as she dressed Naomi for a day of sleigh riding or making snow angels while I stayed behind to salt the walkways and remove snow from the porch roof, so it didn't collapse and now I'll never again have the feeling of being warmed by the image of them returning home, later, from their day out, giggling, smiles stretched across their faces.

That thought alone has my guts doing flips and suddenly I can't remember the last time I ate, but my stomach is telling me it's been a while, so I hit the vending machine a few doors down from my room. I stand in its glow and feed it quarters with my wrapped hand, sucking back drags of my cigarette. I punch in the number code for the candy bar I want and watch the spiral gate retract itself. Before it has a chance to completely draw itself back, it comes to a stop, the candy bar teetering on the edge of the shelf framed within the glass front.

Of course.

I pound on the glass façade with the side of my fist. It does nothing. I resume my attempts by kicking the machine, my anger getting the better of me. But I know it has more to do with what I've let my life become and less about the sugar that is dangling in front of me.

One more attempt with a kick and a punch and a voice comes from somewhere down the sidewalk, past the door of my room.

"Ain't nothing free in life except the advice you don't want."

I act like I don't hear it, keeping myself focused and the voice comes again from the cold dark.

"I think you have to give it money first, mister. I don't believe bullying it into giving you what you want works. Those things can be pretty stubborn."

I squint through the darkness at the shape approaching. When it comes into view, I see it's a woman. She appears young and she walks as if she's gliding across ice. I take a drag of my cigarette and turn my attention back to my efforts at coaxing the machine into giving up the goods, every failed attempt inching me closer to destructive rage.

So, this is how it ends, huh? I fuckin' kill myself over a candy bar.

"Or maybe you're the one that's stubborn." She's closer now and I give in to her attempts at conversation.

"Among other things," I say, not taking my eyes off the prize. "Fuckin' thing is holding my fix hostage."

"You make it sound like drugs."

"Anything and everything can be an addiction," I say, and turn away to face the parking lot, resting my back against the machine.

She is now in full view. Out of the dark and into the glow of the vending machine where we make eye contact and I notice hers are an amazing blue. The kind of blue you could swim in. Mine are becoming a dull green, years of regret having started to weigh down the edges.

She wears a short red dress that hugs her hips in such a way that I can feel my penis aching back from the dead. A black coat rides the curves to the backs of her knees, faux fur lining the collar. Underneath the dress, black stockings that remind me of suicide nets and I can see her skin peeking through. Black boots adorn her feet, and her thick black hair is pulled into a messy ponytail, frayed pieces of hair falling away from it. Her complexion is a beautiful alabaster white with a constellation of adorable freckles shotgun blasted across her face.

"Speaking of addiction, can I bum one of those?" She points to my cigarette.

I flick mine to the parking lot, reach into my pocket for the pack, and remove two. I hand her one, stick the other in my mouth, and fire it up. I watch her dig through her purse, which is seat belted across her chest, and I notice that she already has a pack of cigarettes among the mess inside. I eye her, wondering what her angle is. She's either trying to work me, fuck me, or kill me.

I like this woman already.

She lights the cigarette and says, "So, what's your story?"

"Why do you assume I have a story?"

"Everyone does. Not to mention, you're outside a fleabag motel beating up a vending machine at two AM."

"Just passing through," I say, exhaling streams of smoke, upward and away from where she stands.

She laughs. She does this because she's not buying it and I don't blame her.

I just shrug my shoulders to keep it interesting and she watches me between drags of her cigarette. She notices my hand, sees the blood coming through the thin sheet I have haphazardly wrapped around my knuckles. It's falling away with every drag of the cigarette I take. Makes me think of a beautiful woman taking off her stockings, slowly revealing the goods.

I know the question that's coming. How can it not when such violence is on display? The only thing left to wonder is, do I tell her the truth, or do I dance around it? I mean, I just met this woman. I don't want her to think I'm some kind of lunatic. She doesn't need to know about that part of me. Not yet anyway.

"What the hell did you do to your hand?"

"I punched a mirror."

"What'd ya go and do something like that for?"

"I saw myself in it."

I never was too good at dancing.

She just blinks at me, and my first instinct is to fall in love. She looks like a younger version of my dead wife. They all look like my dead wife. Maybe I just want them to, or maybe I just want them all dead. Maybe I'm pathetic for holding onto something that is no longer real. I don't accept things very well. I always go kicking and screaming like a man being led to the electric chair.

She extends her hand and says, "Name's Analise. Room seven." She throws her head back slightly in the direction from which she came, and our hands meet.

They are soft like sculpted porcelain, and she speaks with a southern accent that'll have me on my knees by morning. This is how it starts. What comes next is the feeling of butterflies, followed by war. Feels like a lifetime since I've been in the presence of a woman. Feels like I've been chasing ghosts for far longer than that.

"Fenton," I say, as our fingers struggle to loosen their grip from one another's.

"Well, Fenton, thanks for the cigarette." She tosses it to the pavement below and stubs it out with a twist of her boot.

We make eye contact one last time and I can suddenly smell the ocean. I close my eyes and taste salt. When I open them, she has turned and is headed back into the shadows, toward her room.

"If everyone has a story, what's yours?" I call out to her.

She points her head upwards but doesn't turn to look at me. "Room seven," she says.

And then she's gone as quickly as she appeared.

Back in the motel room I sit on the edge of the bed and sip from the flask. I have a feeling that holes are being burned into my stomach every time I swallow, and my dick is on edge. It is something I haven't felt since Maddie was alive. I want to go back. Rewind it all and do it again. Some need their past more than others while some spend their whole lives trying to run from it. I'm somewhere in the middle and I feel like a bird waiting for the sky to split me open.

I reach for the phone and undo the receiver from its body and wrap the coiled line around my neck. I lay down on the bed where I crawl miles through my own bad thinking just to find sleep.

CHAPTER: 4

Morning sun through the slit of a curtain—it stabs at my eyelids, heats my face. I roll away from its assault and watch dust dance in a shaft of light. A knock on the door comes like the sounds of war. It rattles the inside of my skull and I'm up and out of bed without a second thought.

I open the door and there's a figure standing in front of me. I squint through the harsh sunlight and realize it's the kid from last night. The clerk from the front desk. He's wearing the same clothes he had on when I checked in. I wonder if he sleeps.

"Sorry to bother you, sir. There was a call for you. I tried forwarding it to your room, but you weren't answering. They said it was important, so they left a message."

He says all this while eyeing the receiver which is dangling in the middle of my chest like a necktie, hanging from the cord that's still wrapped around my neck. I shrug my shoulders, indicating that I don't have an explanation. He hands me the message and says, "Also, we don't serve breakfast but there is coffee in the office area that you are welcome to and there's a diner about two miles that way," he points his finger east, "if you're hungry." I try to look in the direction he's pointing but it's just too bright and I feel like I have knives in my eyes.

I thank him, shut the door, unravel the cord from my neck, and toss it on the bed.

I stand in the middle of the room in just my shirt and boxers and unfold the paper. The message reads: BIT OF A MISHAP. MIGHT BE A COUPLE OF DAYS LONGER THAN ORIGINALLY PLANNED. HANG IN THERE, WE'LL MEET UP SOON.

Shit.

I crumple the paper up, throw it on the floor, and try to rub away a knot forming in my neck.

In the bathroom, I look at a fractured version of myself in the broken mirror, my features distorted and slightly off in a way that makes me uncomfortable although I don't know why.

If I had a soul this is what it would look like.

I've gotten pale. I need sun, followed by a few good nights of deep sleep without dreams. I throw cold water on my face and then drink some from my cupped palms before getting dressed. I grab the duffel bag before leaving the room but leave the gun hidden under the mattress.

The coffee is thick and the color of charcoal. It tastes like acetone going down. I stand outside the motel office and drink it from a paper cup, its steam sloping upward to warm my face against the cold morning air. I light a cigarette and look across the street toward the sound of gunfire—hunters getting an early start. The shots ring out, stirring a cluster of sparrows in a nearby tree. They take off, splitting the sky open in their escape. I watch a circle of carrions, which are set against a picturesque view of the mountains across the street. They ride on an upward stream of wind, and I wonder what died.

There are a few more cars here than there were last night. Must be early morning check-ins. I don't recall seeing them on my late-night excursion and failed attempt at finding food. I glance down the sidewalk toward the rooms of the motel.

Room seven.

I dump the bag in the trunk of my car and, slamming it shut, I get a view of the vending machine. I can see my candy bar still teetering. I think of the asshole who is going to get a two-for-one deal when they drop money in the slot. Whoever it is, I hate them already. It's amazing; the things humans are willing to spill blood over.

From behind the car, I glance over at room seven once more. The seed has been planted and the curiosity is growing. Fuck it, what do I have to lose? Everything important is either already gone or just out of reach. And besides, I don't know how long I'm going to be here. Might as well kill the boredom before it kills me.

I walk to her room and knock on the door.

Analise answers in a t-shirt that is just barely too long. The image leaves me wondering if she's wearing panties underneath it. Her breasts have natural sag. I eye them through her shirt, and she watches me do it. Her hair is pulled back into the same messy ponytail from the night before and a toothbrush hangs from her mouth, toothpaste foaming around the edges of her lips. She looks like a rabid dog in heat, and I want to jump her bones right here and now.

"Fenton." She says my name like she's been waiting for me, and I am just now showing up, late.

"You hungry?"

She smiles.

X X X

The coffee at the diner isn't any better. It tastes like burnt barbecue. Analise and I sit across from each other at a booth in the corner and I wince through every sip. I stab at my eggs with a fork. She eats waffles with her hands and draws long, salacious sips of orange juice through a straw.

"So, Fenton, did you ask me out to breakfast to sit quietly and ruminate, or are you gonna tell me your story?"

Why is she so interested in me?

"Already told you. Just passing through."

"Right, right." She licks syrup from her fingers, and I can feel myself starting to clam up. "I like you," she continues. "Seemingly lonely, but not lonely enough to unload your shit onto the first person who asks. Not too many like you left. Not these days. So many people looking for validation outside of themselves because they're too fucked up to find self-worth on their own. But," she takes a sip of orange juice, "in my experience, a man that starts his car with a screwdriver always has a story to tell."

"I lost my keys. And what makes you think you're the first person to ask?"

She smiles at me and my heart beats like a carnival drum.

"Fair enough."

She finishes her food and pushes the plate away from herself, making room on the table for her elbows. She rests her chin in the palm of her hand and looks at me.

"Don't take this the wrong way, I know we just met and all, but you look like you haven't slept in a year."

It feels like ten, but I don't tell her that. That would only be giving her what she wants and I'm still trying to decide if she's worth giving anything to. Bad enough I'm already paying for her meal.

"Traveling does that," I say and slide my plate to the edge of the table wondering how long this little game of poke and prod will go on. If she keeps smiling the way she does, I'll eventually collapse, and she knows it.

"I know all about that. I ran away from home a few years ago. Got fed up with my daddy…well, my stepdaddy. My real daddy died in a car accident when I was ten. Anyway, I got fed up with him touching me in improper places, you know? I had enough, so one day, as he lay passed out on the couch, I shot him in the temple twelve times with a BB gun. It didn't do anything other than jar him awake from his stupor, but it felt good to mimic the act. Cathartic, in a way."

She pauses and scans my face for signs of life, but she won't find any.

"Anyway, I was halfway out the door before he realized what had happened. I haven't been back since. That was four years ago now. I kind of feel bad leaving my momma there alone with him, but she was the one who thought it wise to marry that piece of trash in the first place, so I suppose that's on her."

"And is all this your way of seeking validation outside yourself?" I sink further into the seat, now slouched and nearly disappearing under the table.

"Kudos to you," she says and claps like she's mocking the rich and snooty.

I take a sip of my coffee and keep my eyes locked on Analise. She has removed her boot. I know this because I can feel her weightless foot in the curve of my crotch. She wiggles her toes and my pecker flutters.

Blood pumping.

Maybe I'm wrong. Maybe she will find life.

"Who is Marciano?" she asks, as she massages the tip of my cock with the heel of her foot.

I look down at the name tag stitched onto my army jacket.

"It's my last name. My father's last name. It's his jacket. He served. I've been wearing this thing a long time and probably more than he ever did."

"Irish face with an Italian last name. Cute."

I don't know how she knows, but she's not wrong.

"Is he still alive, your father?" she asks, letting her foot slide from my crotch and drop to the floor.

"Barely. He was diagnosed with early stages of senility last year and it's just been getting worse. His memory comes and goes. My mother cares for him, but she's getting old herself."

I don't mention that she also takes care of my eight-year-old daughter.

And just like that, she has me talking. It may not be the story she wants, but it's a start and it's only a matter of time before I spill it all.

The entrance bell rings and a cop walks in. Suddenly, I feel like my stomach is about to slip loose from my asshole and spill out onto the diner floor. I try to compose myself, working myself into a fight or flight mentality so I'm ready for whatever comes next. My brain tells me to take the knife I've been using to cut up the sausage links on my plate and slide it up my sleeve.

Just in case you have to stab your way out of here.

I do as I tell myself and watch him as he greets everyone on his way to the only empty stool at the end of the counter.

"You know him?"

"Huh?" I look at Analise, and then back to the cop. "No," I say.

I continue my gaze. He makes idle chit-chat with the waitress and the rest of the locals while I try to listen through the sounds of knives and forks clanking on plates. I listen for anything about the dead guy I left miles back, but I can't hear a goddamn thing.

Do people have to be such savages when they eat?

I wanna fucking scream.

Analise watches me and I realize that I have given her more information in this instant without having to say anything at all. I can feel what little color I have left drain from my face.

"You wanna get out of here?" She asks, sliding her arms into the sleeves of her coat.

I nod and she motions to the waitress for the check. I throw money down on the table without even looking at it and do my best not to draw attention to myself, keeping my eyes fixed on the floor as Analise and I exit the diner.

Outside, clouds are being hauled in piles across the sky, turning the bright morning into a dull wash of dreary grey. I notice a crowd is forming on the street corner a few feet from where we stand. I light a cigarette and watch as a man dressed in a pastor's robe holds up his arms and yells about fire and brimstone to both the people standing in front of him and to those rushing past on their way to and from their morning routines. The robe is sleek, black, and runs the length of his body, stopping just short of his ankles. Silver buttons adorn the front, as well as the cufflinks, while the entire robe itself is trimmed in gold stitching. He stands on a wooden crate, holding a book in his right hand, and when he's done screaming of punishment and salvation, he lowers his hands and holds the book to his chest, tightly, like a child holding a stuffed animal at bedtime.

Naomi.
Maddie.

I feel a writhing in my guts just seeing that book.

"Fuckin' dime-store preachers," I say, throwing up the collar of my jacket to lull the chill that is blowing at the back of my neck.

"I think it's interesting."

"People need religion like they need a fuckin' hole in the head," I say.

"It's no different than anything else in life. At the end of the day, it's just something that keeps you from screaming and completely falling apart. Everyone has a vice."

"My vices don't cause wars," I say and take a pull from my cigarette and glance behind me, keeping my eye out for the cop. I'm expecting him to rush out of the diner and bust me at any moment. "And maybe at the end of the day, I *want* to scream myself to pieces," I continue. "I don't need people tellin' me how to live. Preachers are no different than used car salesmen—they both deal in the art of persuasion and I don't want the bullshit that either of 'em are trying to sell me."

"You seem to be in need of a new car, Mr. Screwdriver," Analise says, tilting her head and smiling, indicating that the comment was meant to be playful.

I stare directly into her eyes for a few seconds and come back with, "Oh, fuck off. I'm leavin'. You wanna ride back or would you rather stay here with the rest of the flock and get served up a plate of bullshit?"

"I'm comin'," she says.

We turn and head for the car and I can hear the Preacher's voice call out to us.

"You two."

Both Analise and I turn and see that he has stepped off the wooden crate. The crowd has parted, giving us a direct view of the Preacher as he begins walking toward us.

"Have you found your lord and savior?"

"Oh, for fuck's sake." I throw my cigarette to the sidewalk.

A beam of sunlight has found its way through the clouds, and it bounces off the Preacher's hair, which is slicked back tightly with natural greases. The light gives off an almost halo-like glow as if someone or something is trying to convince me.

I'm not falling for it.

I grab Analise by the wrist and rush the two of us to the car. She ambles behind me like she's not sure if she wants to go with me or break free and join the cult at our backs.

X X X

Halfway down the road and I feel another headache brewing behind my eyes. I do my best to ignore it, turn to Analise, and say, "What the fuck was that about? He had an entire crowd at his feet, and he singles us out?"

"Correction, I think he was singling you out."

"Alright, the question hasn't changed though."

"Who knows? Maybe he saw something in you that needed saving." Analise smiles another wickedly playful smile from the passenger seat, and she reminds me of a stiletto knife with eyes.

He's not wrong. I need to be saved from myself.

"He's not fooling anyone. I know that talk. Fuckin' jailhouse religion. He's done time."

"What is jailhouse religion?"

"It's the term used for the physiological phenomena where inmates almost always find religion their first time being incarcerated. They relate it to Stockholm syndrome, and it's considered a stress-induced behavioral disorder."

She looks at me with an expression that lets me know she's surprised about what just slipped off my tongue.

"What are you on about, and how does jailhouse religion differ from, like, normal religion, exactly?" She folds her arms across her chest and puts her feet up on the dashboard.

"It's not different in the teachings. That part's the same. It was all in his speech and mannerisms. It wasn't refined as you'd expect from someone who'd dedicated their entire lives to the belief. He spoke it back like he'd arrived at it out of desperation."

She gives me another surprised look and says, "Don't most people arrive at it out of some sort of desperation?"

She has a point.

"I suppose," I say.

"There's definitely more to you than just passing through," she says, staring out the passenger window, sounding mildly distracted by something on the other side.

Eyeing a general store I say, "I need to pick up a few things."

CHAPTER: 5

Brave men run in my family, or so I'm told. This is not something that has been passed down to me through blood, nor was it something I'd been taught. My father, although not a stupid man, was just never good with words. He never bestowed upon me any sort of wisdom or moral code, but rather left me to myself to navigate and figure out how to survive on my own terms. I can't say this is the best way to raise a child, but who am I to judge? Especially when I'm not even raising my own.

Despite all of this, there was one thing my father said to me that rings true, more now than it ever did. It was a few months after I had met Maddie. My father and I were in the garage of my parent's house sharing beers—something we never did until then. I sat in the corner among the discarded lawn mower parts my father liked to tinker with while he sanded down the edges of one of the pine caskets he'd been crafting for my mother and himself.

"There's no way those hucksters are going to take me and your mother for all our savings after we're dead. The prices they charge are criminal. I'll make my own," he said, as he ran his hand along one of the sides, wiping sawdust away from the smooth wood.

Thinking about it now, I believe it had less to do with the money and was more a way for him to deal with his own mortality. He was on the verge of retiring then and he did all he could to keep himself busy. Thinking back on it now, there were signs already beginning to show. At the time though, none of us thought much of it. People forget things, and the more someone does, you shrug it off as part of getting old. It would still be a few more years before it really grabbed hold of him, eating his memories from the inside out, but none of us knew that even he, himself, wouldn't see his own death coming. Which is sort of beautiful in its own way.

I took a sip of my beer and said, "Just throw me in a ditch somewhere when it's my turn to go."

My father laughed. "I hear ya, Fenton. Dead is dead. But I don't think your mother would appreciate either of us being dumped in a ditch. Some people need closure and as strong as your mother is, she wouldn't take to discarding the two most important men in her life in such a haphazard fashion." He blew sawdust from the corner edge of the slat of wood he'd been sanding. "But hopefully she won't have to put you in the ground. No parent should ever have to do that. And besides, I'm only making two of these and they're already claimed, so you might get your wish after all." My father let out a chuckle.

"What does Mom think of you building these?" I asked, reaching into my pocket for a cigarette. I lit it and blew a length of smoke, watching it mingle with the sawdust particles floating.

"She thinks it's a little morbid, but I'm doing it with good reason. Plus, it keeps me busy. I'm gonna do hers up real nice. Maybe put a nice inlay on the lid. Flowers, maybe a Celtic cross to honor the Irish in her." He stopped for a moment and smiled, his eyes going someplace in the past; a memory he didn't share with me. A memory he has no doubt forgotten now. He shook his head, the smile still stretched across his face, "She is all piss and vinegar, your mother."

He threw the sandpaper on top of the casket lid and clapped his hands together, dusting them off. He looked over at me, where I sat slumped in an old lawn chair. There was a look in my father's eyes I had never seen before as if they were about to swell with tears.

"Fenton," he said, "never underestimate the love of a good woman, for she can take the most broken of men and give them the feeling that they have the power to call down rain at any moment. And if you think that love is real, hold onto it with all you've got because her absence will destroy you with the same force she initially convinced you that you had."

It was a bit scary hearing those words come from my old man. He was the kind of guy who didn't express his feelings very often, if ever. I never told my father this, but I admired him. He was old-fashioned, and, like his father before him and along with my uncles, was a hard-working man. Salt-of-the-earth kind of men.

That kind of ideology doesn't exist anymore. Now he's a shell of his former self, his body and mind wracked with age and senility, struggling to hold onto his memories while all I want to do is forget mine. He can barely remember his own name on a good day, and I think maybe he is wiser than I ever gave him credit for. I was wrong all along because he, of all people, found a way to escape his own past. Maybe he will pass something down to me after all. I'd rather not go to my grave screaming and heavy with regret.

I sit on the motel bed and sip the beer I stopped and bought on the way back from the diner. Scattered at my side, across the mattress, are the other items I purchased: Ziploc bags, crazy glue, more aspirin, and various snacks to hold me over because that vending machine can go fuck itself.

I scan the radio for any news involving the body I left behind but hear nothing. I dial it back and find the local station from earlier. Slow jazz leaks from the speakers and I'm already reminded of Analise.

I place the bottle of beer on the nightstand, pop more aspirin, chew it to dust, and take the gun from under the mattress. I open the cylinder and dump the bullets across the sheets.

Six bullet chamber, five bullets remain.

I close my eyes and see blood and bits of skull fragments falling to wet the carpet beneath us. I run my tongue along my teeth. I swear I can still taste his blood and I think, *Poor fucker,* regardless of why he was there. To kill me or not, he didn't wake up that morning thinking he'd find himself on the wrong side of a gun. But then again, neither did I. And really, in a situation like that, which is the right side?

I open my eyes and spin the cylinder of the gun, slapping it shut like a cowboy from all those westerns my father watched when I was a kid. Putting the barrel in my mouth, I grip it with my teeth and feel the cold steel against my tongue. I squeeze the trigger six times in rapid succession, the clicking of the hammer sounding out with every pull.

Analise is right.

It is cathartic.

This is how I survive.

I return the bullets to their chamber and slap it shut once more before dropping it onto the mattress. I pick up the phone and dial my parents' house. On the third ring the last voice I'd ever want to hear answers, sounding annoyed.

"Hello?"

"Hey."

"Where the fuck are you?" My sister's voice comes through in hushed anger.

I ignore the question. "Is Mom there?"

There's silence and for a moment I think we've been disconnected. But then my sister's voice comes back, stronger, more hostile.

"You're working for that scumbag again, aren't you? You've *been* working for him?"

My sister always had a mouth on her, as well as the ability to see right through my bullshit without me even having to speak. Hell, I didn't even have to be in the same room as her. It's probably the reason for my disliking the woman.

"Angie, just put Mom on the phone." And before she has a chance to speak, I cut her off. "What are you doing there anyway? Doesn't Mr. Full-of-Himself expect dinner on the table when he gets home," I say, referring to her husband.

"You got a lot of nerve asking me that. Let me update you. I'm here because you're not. You left Naomi here knowing full well Mom had enough on her plate taking care of Dad, and now I have to take on the responsibility because you won't grow the fuck up. And as for John, at least he provides for his family."

"You know he cheats on you, right?" I say like a smug child. I light a cigarette while I wait for her response, but she stays silent. It's my only weapon against her and like a coward, I use it when she speaks the kind of truths I cannot handle.

I take a drag of my cigarette and say, "Have you told Mom?"

"About?"

"About me being up to my old tricks?" That's as much of a confession as she's getting from me. Not that she needs one.

"Of course not. She has enough she's dealing with. It would be the nail in her coffin."

"Thanks."

"I'm not doing it for you, asshole."

"Well, thanks anyway."

"You're a real fuckin' piece of shit, you know that?"

"Mmhmm," I say, not only because I don't have the energy to argue, but also because part of me believes it.

Angie lets out a sigh and my ear is suddenly filled with the sounds of scraping and crackles as the phone is set down on a table. Moments later, I hear my mother's voice.

"Fenton?" She says my name like she's about to cry.

"Hey, Mom."

I feel bad for my mother at this moment. More than I ever have in my entire life. A woman who no doubt wanted something different for herself, but strong enough to accept the hand that life dealt her and never let that get in the way of her loving her family or doing what was best for them. She's carried more than her share in her lifetime and here I am shoveling more onto her by leaving her to care for my daughter and my father.

"How are you?"

"Where are you, Fenton? When are you coming home?"

As with Angie, I don't have an answer.

"How's Naomi?" I drop my cigarette in the beer bottle and hear the cherry sizzle out and I watch smoke unfurl itself from the bottleneck.

"She's good, but she misses you. She got the lead in the school play. She says she's going to be an actress."

Hearing this fills my chest and for a second, I don't want my heart to stop beating, ever.

"Do you wanna talk to her?" My mother asks. I know she's hoping that I will and that doing so will make me come home and she's right, but it's also precisely why I refuse. Going back now will only make things worse for everyone, especially Naomi.

There's still time for her. She's young enough and bright enough to come out clean on the other side. I've taken too many punches to deal with all of it in any healthy way. The dreams are too frequent now and getting closer. Exposing her to this lifestyle will ruin her. It's not what Maddie would have wanted.

"How's Dad?" I wave lingering cigarette smoke from my face.

"Not great. The doctors say he doesn't have too much longer. He's in rapid decline." She changes the subject, her voice sounding more desperate than when she speaks of my father's declining health. "Fenton, you have to come home. You can't keep hiding. You're going to have to deal with this. Naomi has enough problems with Maddie dying and all, she can't lose you too. Her death has been hard on all of us. None of this is your fault."

If my mother only knew.

"Tell Naomi I love her. Dad too. I love all of you. Even Angie." I hang up the phone and become overwhelmed with the sudden urge to break the beer bottle on the edge of the nightstand and open my own throat.

CHAPTER: 6

Love is the worst kind of suicide in that it only kills pieces of you and never the person as a whole. When it's over, all you're left with are the worst parts of yourself peering back. It's amazing how much of oneself a person can lose without dying. Self-realization can be a fucking terrible thing.

"It will hurt for a while, but it will not end you."

Maddie's voice comes from somewhere inside of me and using the knife I lifted from the diner, I carve a channel into my left shoulder, releasing the endorphins in my brain that have convinced me I feel better when I mutilate myself, if only for a short time.

Where am I in my grief? Does it ever go away, or is it something you just learn to live with? I use a song that Maddie loved as a mental gauge to map how far I've come and how much further I have left to go before I am free of all this guilt-ridden weight. I close my eyes and mouth the words to myself. The further along I can make it without breaking down, the better I am dealing with it. I can barely make it to the second verse before I am destroyed all over again, that last lingering image of her body wrapped in bloody rags seared into my brain.

There is no heaven, but hell is my own bad thinking.

I pull down the sleeve of my t-shirt, letting the fabric soak up the blood.

There's a knock at the door followed by Analise's voice telling me to come outside. I put the gun in one of the Ziploc bags I bought and dump it in the toilet tank before meeting her out front, duffel bag slung over my shoulder.

"What's up?" I zip up my coat to stave off the cold air enveloping us. I put my hands in my pockets.

"Do you feel like company?"

I shrug my shoulders to let her know that I don't care either way.

"Follow me then."

She leads me down the front sidewalk to her room. She opens the door, and we enter. The first thing I see is a bird perched atop the television set, which is turned on but is playing nothing but static with the volume turned down.

"Is that a fuckin' chicken?"

"A rooster, to be exact, but a bird just the same. But don't tell him that." She puts her hand to the side of her mouth like a divider and whispers, "Napoleon doesn't know."

"Napoleon?" I say as I step further into the room, leaning slightly away from the TV with caution as I walk by.

Analise laughs. "He's not going to bite you." She walks toward the bathroom and when she reaches the threshold, she turns around to face me and says, "You two play nice, I'll be out in a minute. And Napoleon," she shifts to meet the bird eye to eye and shakes her index finger at him, "Don't you move from that spot." The door closes and I'm left wondering how the fuck she trained a bird.

I sit in the corner chair, duffel bag between my feet. Aside from the rooster, the room is the exact same layout as mine, but slightly cleaner. I hear the faucet turn on in the bathroom. I'm waiting for Napoleon to go mad and tear the place to shit.

Analise exits the bathroom in just her underwear and a mismatched bra—purple and blue. Her mascara runs in streaks down her face. She's made no attempt to wipe it from her cheeks. Her hair remains in the same messy ponytail it has been in since I met her.

She walks to the dresser and fishes a pack of cigarettes from her purse, slipping one from the box. "Napoleon here," she points to the bird with the cigarette she has pinched between her index finger and thumb, "He's the Muhammad Ali of birds." She fires it up and exhales a slim stream of smoke that immediately fills the room.

I look at her with an expression that I imagine questions her sanity, but I'm intrigued.

She leans against the dresser with one arm across her chest and places her hand in her armpit, while the other delivers the cigarette to and from her lips. I try my best to keep my eyes locked on her face, but they keep straying to the other areas she has exposed, no doubt to unravel me into a soupy mess. She wants something, but I don't know exactly what yet. I'm still trying to figure that out.

I light a cigarette of my own and watch our smoke mingle in the center of the room.

"After I ran away from home, I was homeless for a bit. I did some work for a fella who raised roosters for cockfighting. When I had saved up enough and decided I wanted to move on, he told me I could take a rooster of my choosing with me as a bonus. I had already named him, so naturally, I took Napoleon."

She walks to the bed and sits on the edge of the mattress, and I watch her panties climb up the crack of her ass.

What am I doing? Who is this woman? She's probably going to stab me to death and I'm probably going to let her do it.

Her back is facing me, but she continues to talk, angling her head upward every so often to blow smoke at the ceiling. "So anyway, I was back out on the street but had Napoleon to keep me company this time. I read to him from books I don't remember the names of. My stomach hurt; my feet were dirty. I bathed in rainwater that had collected in empty garbage cans. When I ran out of money, I ate cold ravioli from cans I would steal from various grocers because one of the first things you learn when living on the street is that eating from the trash is the homeless version of Russian roulette. I taught myself to play the banjo after winning one in a game of street cups. Eventually, I entered Napoleon in some local cockfights, and he made us a killing. He became something of a local legend…"

She continues to talk but her voice falls to echoes inside my head and all I can hear now is the tormented crows of roosters being led to slaughter by way of blood sport; the frantic flapping of wings as a crowd of onlookers scream and yell, all because they have money riding on death.

The things we will participate in for money.

Analise glances over her shoulder at me and smiles and for a moment I forget that I'm dying.

"You alright?" She turns to face me, one foot on the bed, the other planted on the floor.

I tell her I'm fine, but I can't imagine that I sound too convincing.

"So, you gonna tell me what it is you do?" She stretches herself across the mattress, belly down, and stamps out her cigarette on the bedside table ashtray that is closest to me. I eye her eloquent form as she lifts the lower portion of her legs in the air, bending them at the knees, and rests her bare feet against one another, the tips of her toes aimed for the heavens. She leans on her elbows and places her chin in her hands, her fingers framing her face.

"I'm a driver."

"For?" She blinks.

I don't answer.

"I'm assuming it has something to do with the bag at your feet. You carry that thing everywhere it seems. Must be something important."

I look at Napoleon atop the television set, watching Analise's movements from the corner of my eye. Sucking back one last drag, I stub my cigarette out in the ashtray.

"So, what's in it?"

"I don't know."

She laughs. "So, you drive things around like some kind of delivery boy and you don't even know what you're schlepping?"

"I don't get paid good money to be nosey. But if they are ever in the market for nosey drivers, I'll drop your name." I take a flask from my pocket and have a drink before holding the flask out, offering her some. She shakes her head in protest.

"You're not the least bit curious?"

"Of course I am, but I know better, so the answer is 'no,' you cannot look inside."

She rolls onto her side and her legs crawl the length of the bed. I watch goosebumps form along the uppermost part of her legs. If I start at her feet and follow them upward, I just might find what I'm looking for. And that's exactly what I'm afraid of.

"What about your wife?"

I didn't mention Maddie, how does she know?

She must see the confusion in my face because she says, "I saw the indentation on your finger. Figured it was from a wedding ring. So, maybe an ex-wife? Am I wrong?"

I run the tip of my index finger along the base of my ring finger. Ten years of marriage and the ring has cut a groove deep into my skin. Ten years and I never took it off, not once. Now it hangs on a string, along with Maddie's, looped around a rusty nail in a place I will never speak of. There is a note for Naomi on where to find them in the event that something should happen to me.

"I'll be working out this dent for a long time to come."

"Wanna talk about her?"

"No."

"What's she like?"

"She was beautiful. A thunderstorm of a lover," I say, because despite telling her I don't want to talk about her, I do. I always do. And I never want to stop.

"Sounds enticing. What happened?"

"I killed her."

"For real?" She sounds more intrigued than she does frightened at the possibility that she could be sitting in a motel room with a murderer.

I did murder someone, just not my wife.

"Not directly, but it was my actions that put her in the situation that ended her life. At least I think so. So yes, I killed her."

"I'm sorry."

"Don't say shit like that. Save your sympathy for someone who is dying of cancer. This is my doing and I have to own it."

"Sounds to me like you're punishing yourself."

She knows me already.

"Someone has to be held responsible, if not the person that did it then the next best thing will have to do. I have no choice but to carry it, otherwise, her death means nothing."

This conversation is getting to me. I have the sudden urge to cut out my own liver and feed it to her as a symbolic gesture of the affection that is growing between us. I've always had a thing for women who back me into corners, leaving me with nothing but my own rage as the only way out. It's a game I'm always willing to play, despite being on the losing end most of the time.

Analise lifts herself up from the mattress and balances on her knees, walking to the edge and calling me over with a slight movement of her finger, strands of her hair now falling away from her head and crab clawing the sides of her mouth. It is an image I cannot resist.

Those eyes. Goddamn, those fucking eyes.

Standing in front of her, she lifts my shirt up and over my head and arms and she sees them. The tiny slivers in my skin. She is seeing me for the first time and she's not looking away. Maybe there is hope.

She presses her fingers into the divots that run along my rib cage. "Jesus, Fenton. Some of these are deep enough to hold water," she says.

I think that to be a beautiful image. Her head tilted to the side, lapping rainwater from the scars I've inflicted on myself due to self-blame and the kind of rage and sadness that has nowhere else to go.

I play with her breasts and slide a hand down the front of her panties—to the place where she grows a minor forest—and feel for the heat. I resist at first but eventually give in and when I do, it's as if she forcibly sucks two fingers into herself with sheer will. I do not kiss her. I have rules. If we start playing that game, we're likely to eat each other alive.

She tells me to lie on my back and I do so, exposing my naked belly to the cool air of the motel room. She kisses my stomach. Runs her lips in a circular motion around my belly button and I'm reminded of dogs in the park. How they'll roll over to expose their genitals to one another, vulnerable but willing no matter the outcome. Her hand moves from my stomach to my zipper. I fix my gaze on the water stains mapping the ceiling. Little islands. Unmarked territory waiting to be found. I wonder if this is how explorers felt before the big discovery.

She takes me in her mouth and sucks me like she's stealing gas—nearly fucks me back to life.

CHAPTER: 7

I dream of Maddie.

It's a desperate dream fed by my own unhinged sorrow. We are standing in the living room of the house we shared, but it's empty like it was after she died. After I cleaned it out. And instead of the normal windows we had, they've been replaced with stained glass like that of a church. She is standing, facing away from me, but I can tell she's been crying. Her back is amassed with bullet holes. I reach out to touch them but then stop myself.

"Remember when you loved me?" I say, taking a few steps back, my arm still extended outward.

Her voice comes from somewhere down the hall and not from the figure standing before me. "I still do."

"Not in the way that matters."

"All love matters, Fenton. Even the fleeting kind."

Now I am crying, tears streaming down my face and I hang my head in shame.

"I miss you terribly," I say.

"I know you do, Fenton, but this…" she pauses for a moment, and I feel a tightening in my chest. "…This life, the way you're carrying on, is not what I want for you. This is exactly what I was afraid of."

I struggle through the sobbing that has forced its way out of me, turning my body into a trembling mess. A pathetic sight. "I know, but it's the only way I know how."

"You never had confidence. Never thought you were capable of doing better, but you are, and you have Naomi to think about."

She's smiling now. I can feel it. I hang my head in shame and wipe tears from my face.

"You're wrong you know," Maddie says.

"About?"

"About me not loving you in a way that matters. But, if you love, you lose. That is the rule."

I look up at her. I want to hold her one last time and never let go.

Down the hall comes the caterwauling of a crying baby. The sound reaches us, filling the room and rattling the windows in their fixtures. I feel like they'll shatter.

I have to go, Fenton. She's hungry."

"She's always hungry. She never stops crying out. Not even in my dreams."

"And one more thing," Maddie says, as she turns to face me. "She is not who she says she is."

I wake with Analise in my arms. It is still dark out. I can see through a slit in the curtain, which is set against the glowing neon sign out front. We're still in her motel room. I know before I open my eyes because she sweats and when she does, she smells vaguely of almonds. It fills my nose and throat before I've fully forced myself from sleep. My stomach feels like a bowl of acid from too much drinking, not enough food, and having to live another day without Maddie. Another day of a life I no longer want.

I pull my arm out from under her and gently roll her away from me. I eye the cluster of freckles that crawl the length of her pale white shoulder line. I walk them with my fingers, and I'm reminded of fresh animal tracks in the snow.

There was a scuffle here and something died.

When you're with someone long enough, you learn that your favorite parts of them are the parts they like the least about themselves; a breast that is slightly smaller than the other, an ass which she thinks is too fat. Even a spattering of blemishes tossed across the skin become the things our fingers yearn for in the dark. Women are too easy to worship. All of them. Because they have something—a curve, a secret—that men are desperate to get at. But I can't worship. Not anymore. That's how religion starts and that's when it all collapses in on itself.

I flip onto my side and stare into the dark. I have no sense of space or distance when waking from dreams. The walls could be ten inches from me or ten feet. I reach out to feel for anything that might save me from myself.

Nothing.

I wonder if she has a body under the bed or a knife hidden between the box-spring and the mattress. I wonder when she's going to kill me. I force myself back to sleep, eager to find out.

CHAPTER: 8

Nothing is forever and people are the biggest gamble. When you first meet someone, you never think, *I'm just borrowing them,* but that's exactly what it comes down to. Ten years later, you find yourself pacing the floor of a hospital watching them slowly slip off into the darkness while down the hall, the universe is balancing things out as a baby is being pushed from its mother. Then you bury what is left, if anything is left of them, and you lose yourself in drink. You spend the rest of your life occasionally looking at pictures of the dead trying to conjure up memories, but it only gets harder as time goes on, eventually resembling nothing but a back alley of ash and cinder.

I wake with the taste of Analise on my lips and the feeling of a stranger's blood pumping through my veins. I want to burst open and thrash around in my own guts. I am too heavy with the choices I've made and the consequences they've laid bare, and I don't know if I'm haunted or just plain crazy, but is there really a difference?

"You seemingly have a lot of trust." Analise stands in the doorway of the bathroom brushing her teeth. She turns to spit in the sink and when she's done, she lies down next to me using her folded arms as a pillow. She blinks at me. "I could have easily killed you in your sleep last night."

Hearing this makes my penis swell. It is words like these that make me think true love exists.

"Don't threaten me with a good time," I say, rubbing a night of bad dreams from my eyes. I roll over and feel for my flask on the bedside table.

"Little early for that, don't ya think?"

This is how I survive.

I ignore the question as I continue my search through the mess of discarded cigarette packs and bitten off corners of condom wrappers.

"While you're over there can you dip into my purse and get my cigarettes? Should be a fresh pack in there."

I take a hit from the flask and say, "I don't go through women's purses."

"What?"

Another hit from the flask and I repeat myself.

"Wanna tell me why?"

"Just a personal rule."

"You'll root around between my legs after knowing me all of twelve hours, but you won't grab the cigarettes from my purse?"

"Not the same thing."

"How do you mean?"

"A purse is a gateway into a woman's life. It's too easy to learn something you don't want to know or something you don't have business learning in the first place. The stakes are just too high and I'm not willing to bet against the odds."

"You're a strange one, Fenton, but I like you."

Hearing her say this makes me uncomfortable. I don't want her admitting anything to me, least of all her feelings.

She slides to the edge of the bed and folds herself in half, reaching for her clothes on the floor. I can see the knots of her spine through her skin. I extend my hand out to touch them and I can't help but feel that I still have glass in my knuckles. I pull back, thinking that it would be too soon for such a gesture. I don't want her thinking I'm falling in love. Or maybe I don't want to admit to myself that it's a possibility. Even though Maddie's gone, it still feels like cheating. She may be a phantom limb now, but the guilt is still present and as strong as ever.

Analise removes herself from the bed completely and steps to the window. She draws back the curtain, letting in razor sunlight, and my eyes scrape the inside of their sockets trying to adjust.

Somewhere outside, gunshots sound as hunters troll the frozen morning in search of food for winter—men desperately hoping they'll stock their freezers with enough meat to keep their families fed through a long winter of little work and even less hope, while I lie in this motel bed trying to figure out what this woman sees in me. Sometimes the mystery is the most beautiful part, other times it's the thing that puts you at the edge. We all have things that keep us alive when really, we should all just lie down and die.

Napoleon is still on the television. He sleeps and I can hear him cooing softly through it. She walks over to him and pets him on the head, then bends forward to apply lipstick in the TV's reflection. I watch her ass through her dress. Two perfect eggs. I am pitifully drawn to her like a moth to a flame and I'm all too eager to fly headfirst into the fire.

Pussy is a gateway drug to emotional ruin and I. Am. An addict.

"You left your blood between my legs last night," she says, still bent forward and running a tube of lipsticks along her lips.

I look down at my shirtless self. I see some of my cuts have opened and there are trickles of dried blood across the sheets.

"Gotta watch that, it could kill you," I say.

"Why do you say that?"

"You don't know what's in it."

"I'm not afraid of dying, but I like your attempt at putting a slip of worry in my head. It's a turn-on."

"Good to know."

"Are you?" She looks over her shoulder at me then turns back to her reflection before continuing. "Afraid of dying?"

"Not as much as I am of being sober." I take another shot and say, "I'll be careful next time, regardless of your lack of trepidation."

"There's gonna be a next time?"

"I suppose."

"You're so fuckin' romantic I could explode."

She stands and smacks her lips together to even the spread of blood-red lipstick and it looks like she's bitten off the head of the rooster. I smile at this image and sink further into the bed. I pull a cigarette from a pack and stick it in my mouth.

Analise crosses the room. She stands before me at the foot of the mattress and asks, "How did she die?"

She's serious. She wants to know, but the answers don't come clean and quiet. Not anymore anyway, and certainly not the ones that matter.

I talk around the filter of the unlit cigarette.

"It's not important."

"What is then?"

"Love, I suppose."

"Define love."

My eyes flutter upward as if I'm trying to look inside my own skull for the answer. "Love is not unlike a religious experience, which in turn I would define as everything I don't understand."

"Interesting."

"Problem is, it never seems to last long enough."

"What is enough?"

"Enough is never enough." I take another drink, first removing the still unlit cigarette from where it dangles loosely from my bottom lip.

"Wait, what are we talking about? Are we talking about love or drinking? You're confusing me."

"Both, I suppose. Maybe neither. I don't know."

"Well, the only thing drinking this early is good for is putting you into an early grave."

"Back to this, are we?"

"Just sayin'."

"And so what if it does? If this is what keeps me going," I hold the flask up, "what's the big deal? We all live until we don't. So, if drinking keeps me alive until I die, what's the harm?"

"There's a kind of poetry to that. The thing that keeps us alive is the thing that will ultimately end us. I like it, but some would argue that it's not about dying but about the quality of life you live before *you* die."

I light the cigarette and take a drag. "Quality is overrated," I say, staring into the flame of my lighter and exhaling smoke.

"What a juvenile response to a serious comment," she says and pulls at a piece of dry skin on her lip. I watch her flick it to the room. Maybe later I'll get on my hands and knees and search for it, put it under a microscope, get a glimpse of her biological makeup, and find out what kind of creature she truly is. "You're avoiding something," she continues, "and I get the sneaking suspicion you've been this way your whole life."

"Let's say you're married," I say and pull my eyes away from the flame and set my gaze on Analise. "And it was *you* that saved your husband from a life that would have ultimately killed him or, at the very least, would have eaten up a good chunk of his life spent behind bars. Let's say you saved him from either of those things. And then let's say that because of certain things beyond anyone's control, he begins to slip back into those things you saved him from, but the only reason he's returned to it is to ensure you don't go hungry or homeless. Now, the return to this lifestyle brings with it other bad habits that he'd also left behind when you married him. For instance: drinking. And he drinks because the job is heavy. It has the potential to be dangerous too and the consumption of alcohol is the only way he knows how to deal with what life is throwing at him. The hours are demanding, you never see him anymore, but it's the only way to keep you fed and sheltered. How does this make you feel?"

"Where is this suddenly coming from?"

"Just answer the question. How would this make you feel?"

"I can't answer the question, but not for the reasons I'm assuming you want me to."

"Why not?"

"Because the question you're presenting is a hypothetical and I hate hypotheticals. For me to answer truthfully, I'd have to have been in that exact situation and I wasn't, so I can't answer it. I could only answer it from a superficial standpoint, thus making the answer meaningless and you're not looking for meaningless. You're seeking something with weight."

She looks to me for something and when I don't give her what she expects, she says, "I'm not your wife, Fenton. I can't answer this question, I'm sorry."

There's a heavy silence for a few moments. The kind of silence you have no choice but to reflect in, and in this moment, I can feel it kill what little ego I have left.

"A fuckin' church of all places." My eyes go someplace else as I continue. "Maddie had no business being there. We weren't religious, never have been. I wanna assume she was at a loss and that she feared for my safety, or even hers and Naomi's, and the only thing she could think of was to pray. But she wasn't praying because she was found in the confessional booth." I stop myself before continuing and force back the tears welling up behind my eyes.

If I start crying, I may never stop.

"The guy entered through the front like everyone else," I say, my voice falling to whispers. "That's what the ones who survived said, and there weren't many of those. Everyone in there just assumed he was there for the same reasons as anyone else. When you wake up in the morning, you don't think your life is going to change *that* much, but it doesn't work like that." I take a few, slow drags, from my cigarette before I continue. "He unloaded a semi-automatic rifle into the small crowd of people gathered inside, fucking pieces of them falling away from their bodies. Turned the confessional booths into Swiss cheese, and my wife along with 'em. And when the gun was empty, he walked through the crowd of bodies puncturing holes in what little was left of them with a fuckin' screwdriver. Left the thing embedded in Maddie's neck. She hung on nearly twelve hours, and the fucked up part is while she's lying in a hospital bed trying to cling to life all I wanna do is ask her why she was in a church in the first place. And even worse than that, I don't wonder why the guy did it. That kind of anger, the kind that pushes you to such extreme acts, I get it. I've been living with a similar rage my entire life, but what I can't figure out is what the fuck she was confessing.

Whatever it was, it must have been some sin because she lost her life over it."

I look at Analise. Her eyes are wet. The cherry of the cigarette I'm holding is damn near down to the filter. I can feel the heat edging toward my fingers and I'm just waiting for the sear to cinch itself around my knuckles.

"So, you were right," I say, admitting defeat, "About there being more to the screwdriver stuck in the ignition of my car. There has to be some satisfaction in that at least."

"I don't find satisfaction in anything you just told me. It's horrible and I couldn't even begin to imagine, nor will I try to find words to comfort you, because those kinds of words simply do not exist. But what I will say is this: We all have secrets, Fenton. If we offered up everything to everyone then we'd have nothing left for ourselves."

"And yet you have your answers, but I still don't have mine." I eye the frost forming on the window. It's getting colder out there. Not long now before we enter a dead winter. My chest tightens up at the thought. I don't know if I can make it through a winter without her.

I look to Napoleon, then to Analise. "I've never understood worshiping in such open places," I say. "Like big churches and cathedrals, you know? Always seemed so impersonal to me. Like your voice would just get lost somewhere inside, trying to find the ears it was meant for. Just voices turning to echoes only to get lost in the architecture and haunt it for all time. Maybe that's what ghosts really are; not disembodied spirits, but the cries for help that were never answered."

"Have you ever seen a ghost?" Analise says with sudden vigor, as if I've just tapped into a hidden interest very few people knew she had.

Every time I close my eyes.

"No. I don't believe in that sort of thing, I'm just talking." I stub the cigarette out in the ashtray and continue. "We used to do this thing, Maddie and me. She'd lie on her side, and I would lightly run my fingers along her back. It helped her fall asleep. But sometimes, I would spell words with the tip of my finger, and she'd have to guess what the word was. It's things like that I miss most."

Analise crawls into bed and nestles up to me. She lays her head on my chest and looks up at me with eyes that say, 'I want to save you, but only you can save yourself.' But the only way to do that is to deal with all of this and I'm afraid that if I learn how to live without her, my time with her will have meant nothing.

"And how is any of this *not* important?" she asks me, placing her hand over my heart.

"Because you knowing it, and me saying it doesn't change a goddamn thing."

CHAPTER: 9

I watch them from the front seat. There are two of them and they move like vultures around a car. Opening and closing doors, digging through the trunk. From the parking lot to the check-in office and back again without a single word uttered between them. I eat fast food off the dashboard and smoke a cigarette with the windows rolled up, clouding the inside of the car, and choking myself out.

Tears in my eyes now and I feel like I have insects breeding under my fingernails, scalp, and teeth.

I eye the glove compartment but refrain from opening it. Buried somewhere inside is a picture of Maddie, Naomi, and myself. The only thing I have left of that life. It was taken back when happiness seemed like a possibility. Before everything went to shit in a storm of bullets. It's the only time I can see Maddie without wounds now because every time I close my eyes, she's riddled with holes. I can slip my fingers through them if I want to, but I don't want to. I want to stuff them full of cotton and will her back to life and do it all over again. Tell her I love her, kiss her forehead, and lay with her through a thunderstorm like we used to. Ten years of good memories and the only thing I can conjure up is the image of her in a hospital bed. Hook me up to something and wipe it clean from my head. If I am anything like my father, I hope I get his disease and I hope that is the first thing it cuts from my memory.

They are definitely up to no good. I can see it in the way they walk. They think they're being slick, unassuming, but I know these types. I suppose I am one. They deal in drugs—out in these parts most likely home-cooked meth and prescription pills; OxyContin, commonly referred to as "Hillbilly Heroin"—or under the table gambling; debt collectors for some backwoods bookie. The kind of guy who has all the yokels fooled, thinking that he is King Shit, but who would crumble to his knees having to deal with the real thing outside his little empire of halfwits. Yeah, I know these types. I've dealt with them before making drops and doing pickups.

I count the good deeds I've done on my fingers. I don't need both hands.

I count my teeth with my tongue.

The passenger side door opens, disturbing the thick cloud inside. It dances in ghost-like patterns throughout the interior of the car, like the memory of a former lover, and then leans toward the open door, finally making its escape, leaving behind a thin layer that hangs back.

"Jesus Christ, crack a fuckin' window in here. What are you tryin' to do, kill yourself?" Analise says, sliding into the passenger seat and closing the car door.

I look over at her and she arches her eyebrows, her face taking on an expression that says, "Oh yeah, I forgot who I'm talking to."

I don't remember askin' for company so if you're gonna sit here, shut your bratty mouth," I say, and smile slightly before going back to watching the two figures walk the front of the motel on their way to a room.

"Oh my god, did someone just smile? That's the first time I've seen you do that since I met you. It's a good look for you." She sounds like a sixteen-year-old girl, giddy and adorable.

I fight back another smile and ask, "What did I just say?"

"So bossy. I love it when you talk to me like that." She cracks the window a bit, breathes into her palms, rubs them together, and then says, "Whatcha doin' out here in the cold anyway?"

"Watching these two mooks." I point to the guys entering room twelve.

She steals a French fry from off the dashboard and talks around it as she pushes it into her mouth.

"Any particular reason?"

"No. Just noticed them. They look to be up to no good though."

"How can you tell?"

"Just a feeling."

"Are these feelings usually trustworthy?"

"Usually, but it's none of my concern. Just making an observation."

"What're you thinking?"

"Dealers, maybe. Possibly tweekers. The kind of guys who would steal dope from someone and then turn around and use it as leverage to finagle a blowjob from said person's girlfriend."

Analise chuckles. "Oh my god, that's kind of clever." She plucks another fry from the dashboard.

I look at her, a stern glare across my face. I nod my head and then let my expression go slack. "You're right, it is kind of clever." We both laugh.

"I like this version of you. You're starting to loosen up." She swallows the last bite of her French fry then leans her head against the passenger side window and draws lines in the frosted glass. A tic-tac-toe board. The neon sign out front throws pulses of red light against her face and my heart pumps in sync. I eye the glove compartment and for a moment I think about crawling deep inside my own anger and closer to the fire where maybe I can sweat out the affliction.

"X's or O's?" she says, leaning away from the door and looking at me.

And just like that, the past comes back to eat my face.

Most days Maddie was up and out of the house before I was, especially when I started working car gigs for Corsetti again. I was out all night hotwiring and delivering cars to his chop shop and didn't get home until the sun was coming up. Maddie was up every morning with Naomi, feeding and teaching her things like how to tie her shoes and how to read and just being a mother to our daughter. If she left the house before I was up, she always left the same message on the bathroom mirror. Applying lipstick, Maddie would kiss the mirror, leaving an imprint of her lips, and write **LOVE YOU** next to it. When Naomi was old enough to draw lines, Maddie would lift her up onto the bathroom sink and have her sign **XOXO** below it. It was a message I saw nearly every morning for years. A message from my girls, as my reflection looked back at me with regret and shame and a weakness that has kept me from doing anything about it.

A slap on the shoulder brings me back and I hear Analise from somewhere inside the car.

"X's or O's, man?"

I force the memory back into the furthest part of my skull and suddenly I feel the cold more than I ever have up to this point in my entire life. I cross my arms and watch snowflakes form and fall against the windshield.

"Which one's kisses?" I ask.

"What?"

"Never mind."

The guy on the television, whose hair is perfectly sculpted to the point I want to reach into the TV and punch him in the face, says the light snow could turn to a full-blown blizzard in the next twenty-four hours. I watch him deliver the anxiety-inducing news from the check-in desk. If someone doesn't get here soon, I might be held up here for a few more days. I know enough about small towns and how they operate in the winter. They'll just wait for the storm to pass before even attempting to plow a back road like this one, and even then, it's the main roads that are of first concern. I could be here for days after that.

I watch the news for a few more minutes to see if anything is being reported about the man I shot, but still nothing. Maybe I'm in the clear. Maybe my guilt is punishment enough.

I ring the bell and the same kid from the last few days or so shuffles out of the back looking like seven pounds of shit shoveled into a two-pound bag. He looks at me and right away knows exactly what I want.

"No messages, sir," he says, leaning on the desk with his elbow and picking the dirt from his fingernails with a Swiss army knife. "But if you want, I could come directly to you as soon as there is, so we don't have to keep doing this."

The kid has a smarminess to him I hadn't noticed until just now. I would love to knock out his remaining teeth. Teach him a lesson about manners and doing the job he's being paid to do, but something tells me it wouldn't do any good. Besides, the fact that he's been the only one working this desk for these past few days and looking like he's gotten no sleep tells me he's most likely geeked up on something and that means he wouldn't feel the beatdown anyway. I don't bother with a response, I just turn and walk out and head back to my room, making sure not to look at the vending machine on my way by.

I check under the bed for the duffel bag, my paranoia growing every moment I can't leave this place. I do push-ups until my arms burn. I put a sliver in my stomach, the wounds now starting to cross themselves. If I keep this up, I'm going to have to start using my face as a canvas. I pick at the scabs of the ones that are healing.

This is how I survive.

I bounce on my toes and punch at the air like a boxer getting ready for the big fight. I chew aspirin and wash it down with a sip from the flask. I dial out and a few seconds later I'm greeted by a voice that brings it all crashing down.

"Hello?"

"Hey, baby girl."

"Daddy?"

"The one and only."

"Where are you?"

"Working."

"When are you coming home?"

I reduce my voice to a whisper because it's the only way to fight back the tears. "Hopefully soon, baby."

"I miss you."

"I miss you too. Are you behaving for Grandma and Aunt Angie?"

"Mmhmm, but Roscoe smells and he sleeps in my room sometimes. He balls himself up on my clothes that Grandma sets out for school the night before."

She's referring to my parents' cat. I almost forgot about him. How the hell is he still alive? They've had him since I was a teenager.

"He just likes you is all. And he's old. He used to do that to me when I was younger."

"Yeah, but he probably didn't smell as bad."

I laugh through the tears and say, "Probably not."

"When you come home can we go to the ice cream shop that makes the root beer floats with the bananas and whipped cream on top?"

That was our thing before I returned to working for Corsetti. Every Saturday we'd let Maddie sleep in and I would take Naomi for a breakfast of root beer floats, always telling her that it was our secret. If Maddie found out we were consuming nothing but sugar for breakfast, I never would have heard the end of it to which Naomi would reply, "At least it has bananas in it." Then the two of us would look at each other and say in sync, "And some bananas are better than no bananas because at least bananas are a fruit.

"You know it."

"Do you wanna talk to Grandma?"

"No, I suppose I don't. Hearing your voice was enough."

"K," she says, and I can almost hear her face stretch into a smile. The smile which makes her resemble her mother more than anything else.

"But can you do me a favor?" I ask, feeling like a total asshole for asking my daughter to do something for me when all I've done is leave her with feelings of confusion and abandonment. The same way that Maddie dying has left me. "Can you keep this little conversation between me and you?"

"Like root beer floats for breakfast?"

I smile. "Exactly, just like root beer floats for breakfast."

And like always, in tandem we say, "And some bananas are better than no bananas because at least bananas are a fruit."

She giggles and my heart feels like it's going to burst.

"I love you, beautiful."

"I love you too, Daddy."

I hang up the phone and scream into the pillow.

CHAPTER: 10

Learning the truth can lead to two things: solace or a lifelong bender. Never learning it, well, that's a different kind of hell where every day becomes a labor. I know she's gone, but it doesn't keep me from looking. Always expecting to see her face somewhere in a crowd, as if I'll find her and I can say, "There you are. Can we go home now?"

Therapists would say that living in grief is no way to live. That you have to find something that'll help you push through it, but my grief is the only left that connects me to her. If I sever it, what remains? It's a horrible feeling when you don't want to be where you are, but you don't want to be anywhere else either. Is that how Maddie felt? Was she going to leave me?

But she did leave me. And in the worst way possible.

These are the things I think of as Analise talks of her period. She is laying on the edge of the bed, wrapping the coiled telephone wire around her finger. I lay next to her with my hand halfway up her skirt, my mental state slowly falling away from me like chunks of wet bread, and I wish I could chase any fears she may have into the cold outside, but my sympathy is lost somewhere inside me now. Like a sunken stone at the bottom of a lake. I wouldn't even know how to go about retrieving it.

"The first time I got it, I thought God was trying to kill me," she says. "My momma never told me about these things. Nor did anyone else for that matter. It always reminded me of melted cherry popsicles in the summer—still does. I never did eat the last bite. I'd put it on the sidewalk and watch the ants bum-rush the sticky puddle. Sometimes I'd photograph it with the Polaroid camera my daddy got down at Sutter's thrift store. My real daddy, mind you, not that piece of shit I had for a stepfather. My father is also responsible for my love of poetry. He made me recite it when I was a kid because I was really shy and talking in front of people scared me so badly that I would stammer a lot, you know? Anyway, so he would have me read poems aloud to him and with him. The first poem I ever memorized was *Stopping by Woods on a Snowy Evening* and he was so proud of me. He bought me a beautiful picture book. I still have it."

She speaks only of her past and never where she's going. Reminds me of myself and it's exactly the reason I don't fully trust her.

Analise rolls over and straddles me. She fumbles for the zipper of my pants. We tussle and suddenly I'm inside her and we're fucking again, if for no other reason than to stave off the feeling of wanting to die. Sometimes you have to grasp at something, anything, to help you fight your way through the madness.

This is how I survive.

She pulls the shoulder straps of her dress down over her arms, her breasts falling in a weighted reveal, and I smell almonds again. I grab at her thighs and she bucks, her orgasm coming on almost violently and then melting into me, she quivers, and I remember that a quiver is where you store arrows.

When we're done, we resume our positions on the bed. She leans into me. I suck in her breath and just as our lips are about to meet, I pull away.

"Why won't you kiss me?"

And there it is. The question that could potentially undo everything.

"Don't ruin a good thing," I say.

"I'm just curious." She rolls away from me to light a cigarette. She takes a drag and passes it to me.

"I have rules."

"Rules? Oh, so the purse thing isn't your only rule?"

"Of course not. Everyone has rules, don't they?"

"Yeah, but most people's rules are don't steal, don't kill, take your shoes off at the fuckin' door. Stuff along those lines."

"No, no. Aside from the societal rules most people follow, everyone has things they deem acceptable on a personal level."

"Okay. Yeah, sure. But why no kissing? Is it me?"

I laugh. "No, nothing like that."

"Why are you laughing?" She takes the cigarette from me and presses the cherry against the rim of the ashtray she has resting in her lap. She rolls the cigarette by its filter, twisting off the ash that is forming.

"You're just cute is all."

"Why though?"

"Why are you cute? Mannerisms, facial structure…"

Analise cuts me off, knowing I'm trying to stall. "No, why won't you kiss me, wise ass. Tell me." She nudges me.

I let out a sigh. "We're just not there yet," I say.

"How so?"

"Kissing is personal."

"Well, what's fucking then?"

"Sex? Sex is just animalistic nature. An act of violence we all agree on." She stays silent and I take it as a sign she wants a further explanation. "Sometimes sex can just be sex, but a kiss…well, there's nothing sadder than an empty kiss and I don't want any part of that sorrow."

"Let's just leave together. Like right now." Her eyes go wide as she hands me the cigarette. She lays the ashtray between us and rolls onto her side, leaning her head against the flat of her hand.

"I don't think that's a good idea, we barely know each other. Besides, I can't go anywhere until this bag is in the hands of its rightful owner."

"That's a lame excuse," she says, suddenly looking like an eight-year-old girl who has just been told *no* for the first time.

"But it's an honest excuse." I look at her and her eyes are alive with a yearning she never knew existed. "You're serious, aren't you?" I sit upright, leaning away from the headboard.

"I am."

"Let's take it back a notch," I say.

I feel her hand on my neck and she says, "I think I may be falling in love with you."

Is that even possible?

But then again, why couldn't it be? It's not like there's any kind of strict time frame that tells you how long it'll take for you to develop feelings for someone. And you certainly don't choose who you fall in love with. That kind of shit is beyond our scope of understanding. Maddie had a theory that the chemicals in our brains that allowed us to experience love were the same chemicals that caused the big bang, thrusting us into existence. I don't know if I actually believe that, but I always found it interesting and enjoyed the late-night conversations it stirred up with her as we laid in bed.

I rest my back against the headboard again and stare at the ceiling. I take a couple more drags from the cigarette and hold it out for Analise to take. "Don't say that."

"Why?"

"It's a complication I don't need right now."

"Just because it may pose some complications doesn't make it any less true."

"For you."

"I never said otherwise."

Now she's making me feel bad. "And how do you think this is gonna work? You think we're just gonna run off and fall in love and live happily ever after?"

"Maybe. Anything is possible if you open yourself up for those possibilities."

"I have no interest. I've been there and I know what it leads to."

"Such a cynic." She rolls away from me, putting the ashtray on the nightstand and leaving the cigarette burning inside.

"And you're naïve." I lean forward, away from the headboard again, but this time anger and frustration boiling to the surface and fueling my movements. "Relationships are bullshit—romantic or otherwise—and love makes you a fucking hypocrite. It's all pressure. I don't want people to care about me. It'd make it so much easier to let go without feeling regret. You can't even want to die without having to worry about someone else's feelings about it. God forbid you'd want to opt-out and escape all this," I throw my hands up, gesturing to the world. "And when the other goes first—if they, in fact, go first—you find yourself struggling with the feelings that had you resenting the whole concept of love in the first place. Relationships are nothing more than the agreed-upon term that you exclusively fuck one another until one of you is dead or in a mental hospital and loving anyone leads to either."

She stays silent for a few moments, taking in everything I just said. Calmly calculating what her response will be like one should. Reminds me of Maddie.

"I don't disagree with a lot of the things you're saying. It's hard not to when you've lived and have seen all the shit this world can do to a person, and I know you miss her, but there are ways through it." Analise angles herself toward me. Our eyes meet like the first time we met outside by the vending machine. "Life is a gutter, Fenton. The trick is learning to live it lying on your back so you can see the stars."

And maybe she's right. Maybe this is what I need to survive. Maybe this is my shot at a do-over.

"Just don't tell me later that I didn't try." She says, her voice buried now in the pillow.

"Try? Try what?"

"Nothing. Never mind. I'm tired."

I let her fall asleep in silence and when I hear her softly snoring, I slip from the bed and enter the bathroom to put a sliver in my skin and I do it without turning on the light.

CHAPTER: 11

Like always, I can't sleep. I stand outside with my jacket zipped up to my chin. It's still snowing. Light but steady, a thin coat already beginning to blanket the road and parking lot and I watch the only streetlight for miles illuminate the flakes in an amber glow.

Stare too long and it becomes otherworldly.

If I stare too long, I may not want to return.

I smoke and sip from a beer bottle. I fling bottle caps, ones that have been collecting in my pocket for God knows how long, into the cold dark of the parking lot and beyond. I think of Analise and what she said. I think of Naomi. I was wrong. My grief is not the only thing tying me to Maddie. Naomi is a direct line and I hate myself more than I ever have, in this moment, for just now realizing it. What kind of father am I?

I do this for a while—wonder and contemplate, digging myself deeper into the self-loathing pit. It's what I'm good at. It seems to be the only thing I'm good at anymore. Something is nagging at me—something different this time. It pulls at my insides but never reveals itself. I want to scream my heartache into the lazy floods of stars above, but I swallow it instead and keep it down with a few more swigs of cheap beer where it settles in my stomach and turns to fever.

I finish my drink and chain-smoke a few more cigarettes and head back to my room. I reach the door and suddenly someone is behind me pressing a blade to my neck.

"Don't. Fucking. Move." His voice comes through muffled, but with a nervous edge to it.

Despite the threat, I'm impressed. Where did he come from? How did I not hear him with the snow underfoot? Where the fuck was he hiding?

I put my hands up, indicating I'm not willing to get stabbed over whatever it is he's after—not until I find out exactly what it is anyway—but it does nothing to abate the anger that seems to be driving the blade deeper into my neck. I feel my skin lap the tip. This fucker wants blood regardless of whether I'm willing to do what he says. If he only knew what I looked like without a shirt on. Only then would he realize how little the chips he thinks he holds mean.

"Where's the key?" I feel his hand on my shoulder tremble. He wants to be in this situation about as much as I do. Probably even less.

"Front right pocket," I say, "but it's not locked."

"Jacket or pants?"

"What?"

"Are the keys in your jacket or your pants?" He sounds out each word as if I'm mentally deficient and I need him to talk slowly for me to understand.

"Jacket."

"Get the key," he says.

A voice from somewhere my eyes can't reach says, "He just said the door wasn't locked."

"I don't care what the fuck he said, get the goddamn key."

From the corner of my eye, another person comes into view. He's carrying a sawed-off shotgun and wearing a pillowcase over his head with eye holes cut out and I assume that's the reason for the muffled voice at my back. It's the two assholes I watched from my car earlier.

Or was it yesterday? I can't remember.

I knew they were up to no good.

The one with the shotgun retrieves the key from my pocket and turns the doorknob, testing me. When he learns I'm telling the truth, he opens the door and I'm forced inside, knife still in my neck.

We startle Analise awake upon entering. She looks at me and then at the two pillowcase-clad assholes and she pulls the covers to her neck, balling herself up against the headboard.

"What the fuck?" She screams.

"Get dressed," says the one with the knife to my neck.

"What the fuck is going on?" Analise continues trying to climb backward but she's as far as she can go.

"Cut the shit, Analise, it's over. He wants it done and he wants it done now." He talks around the side of my face.

And there it is. The big reveal.

"Friends of yours?" I say.

"Shut the fuck up or I'll open your throat."

But if he's going to, it won't be on purpose, otherwise, he would have already done it.

I watch Analise as her eyes move back and forth between the two mooks and me. I can see her brain working overtime trying to think of a way to make this look good for her. Her eyes lock on mine and she mouths the word SORRY, as if that's all a situation like this needs.

"You heard him," the one with the shotgun says, taking a few steps forward, closer to the bed.

Analise gives up. "Alright, alright," she says like a teenager being told to get up for school for the third time. She slides from the mattress holding the blanket around her torso and heads for the bathroom, picking her clothes up off the floor on her way in.

She exits a few moments later in a dress. Her boots aren't tied. I can hear the laces sweep the carpet as she walks to the bedside table to fetch a cigarette. I watch her hips. Even in our current situation, I want to get lost in the tangles of her hair and feel her pale skin on my lips and I realize from the silence in the room that the other two are thinking the same thing.

"I don't know what this is about, but I can assure you I don't have anything that would be of any value to you," I say, breaking the awkward silence.

"You have more than you know," says the one with the shotgun as he takes a seat on the corner edge of the bed. He's heavier than the one at my back—that much I can tell. Stocky, but almost no muscle. He wears pants held up by a belt but not even that is doing much for him because the pants are still loose in the crotch and look like they're ready to slip right off his ass. He also wears a thick, black, and grey checkered flannel shirt that seems to be a size too small, his stomach ready to blow the buttons off the damn thing, and underneath the pillowcase, I can tell his head is the size of a pumpkin.

"If you're referring to the bag, I can't let you have it. It's not mine to give away."

"I thought I told you to shut up. We aren't here for any bag, dipshit." He gives me a little shove but doesn't release the pressure that is still building behind the blade.

"What's with the pillowcases?" Analise lights a cigarette, avoiding making eye contact with me as she does.

"It seemed fitting for the occasion," the guy at my back says like he's just now realizing how ridiculous it is.

"I didn't know hostage situations were an excuse to play dress up. It's like a fashion show in here." Analise strikes a pose, cigarette dangling from her lips, and I smirk. "Anyway," she continues, "isn't it a bit late for that? He's been looking at my face for the last few days."

"I'm not in the mood for your jokes, Analise."

"Says the guy dressed like he's auditioning for the KKK."

"Now I done told you once. Next smart-ass comment that comes out of you is gonna be met with a fist to that fuckin' mouth of yours. And don't think I'm playin'. I'll knock those prissy perfect teeth out so all you'll be good for is suckin' fluids through a straw and gummin' dick."

"It's true, Darnell," the second man says from the edge of the bed, shotgun now resting on his lap.

"Oh, hell. Now he knows my fuckin' name, you asshole."

"He's already seen her face, what does it matter?" He shakes his head and I think it might roll right off his shoulders from the sheer weight of it. "I agree with Analise, it just seems pointless now. Plus, it's hot in this thing." He pulls the pillowcase from his head and throws it to the floor. His skin is the color of muted bone—almost grey— and clean-shaven. The hair on his pumpkin-sized head is dirty and uneven like he cut it himself with safety scissors meant for first-graders. His eyes are set deep in his enormous skull and rimmed with dark circles like he hasn't slept in weeks, and I wonder what keeps a guy like this up at night.

"Yeah, you really didn't think this through, did you, Darnell," Analise says, making sure to emphasize his name.

"For fuck's sake, will everyone just shut the fuck up? What is up with you two tonight?" Darnell looks to Analise, then to the heavyset one sitting on the bed. "This operation has turned into a real shit show. Shall we all have a little sit-down and formally introduce ourselves?" He sucks in air and lets it out slowly, no doubt to calm the growing frustration. "Harlan's pissed," Darnell says. "There's a lot of money riding on this one." He grips my shoulder tighter and nudges me in place. "More than usual. The whole plan should have been put to bed days ago, but you just had to go and fall for this one, didn't ya, Analise?" He's distracted now and he slips up because I feel the tip of the blade retract and I take my chance.

I throw my head back, into his face, and hear a crunch like glass underfoot as his nose breaks against the back of my skull. I get loose from his grip as Analise picks up the ashtray from the nightstand and cracks the other one over the head with it. It only stuns him, but it's enough for her to wrestle the shotgun loose from his hold on it.

I turn to face Darnell. I see a blot of red blooming through the pillowcase. He swings the knife and I catch him by the wrist, cutting myself in the process. I yank him off balance, setting him up for a right hook. I throw a fist and make contact with the side of his face, throwing the pillowcase out of alignment. The punch doesn't drop him, but it knocks him back against the door as he claws at the slip casing he has yanked over his head to regain his sight. Behind me, I hear the groans of the second mook and the rack of the shotgun.

CHAPTER: 12

Out behind the motel, under the grey wash of dawn, lays an expanse of briar patches and dead trees, their limbs resembling arthritic fingers warning of bad weather coming. I walk behind Darnell and the other, whose name is Yusuf, pointing the knife that was held to my neck an hour earlier at their backs. I corral them to the right of Analise who stands facing all three of us, shotgun aimed and ready to blow a God-sized hole through their stomachs.

The snow continues to fall, getting heavier, but still not the blizzard the weatherman is predicting. I look above and see clusters of widowmakers lying in wait to deal their damage and it is at this moment that I see only two options. One, I can help Analise kill these two lowlifes, regardless of not knowing the full extent of what is going on between the three of them, in which I somehow play a role, and go back to the motel with her where I'll continue to squeeze what little life I have left out of my miserable existence. Or two, I can throw the knife down, letting this little ménage-a-trois play itself out and lay down in the woods, letting my body get lost to the impending storm until spring, at which point the birds will wrench themselves from the thawing freeze to pick my bones clean.

I wrack my brain for a third option but find nothing.

"So, how do you wanna do this?" Analise asks, taking a spot next to me and resting the shotgun on her shoulder.

"Me? You're running the show here and if I'm gonna be honest, I'd rather not do it at all, but letting them go isn't an option either, seeing as they threatened to kill me and all."

"Well, in all fairness, you do wanna die anyway."

"It's my nature." I shrug my shoulders.

"What is, wanting to die?"

"Wanting something but refusing it when someone offers it up on a silver platter."

"And therein lies the struggle."

I nod my head in agreement.

"Why do you think that is though?" Analise asks.

"Not sure. Maybe death shouldn't come so easily. Like most things in life, it should be earned."

"I think you mean that you haven't punished yourself enough."

"Could be. My entire life I've loved with the same passion that I hate. The problem is I've always hated more than I've loved, and I've always hated myself more than I've loved anything else."

"Oh, for the love of fuck. Gimme the gun, I'll shoot myself. Standin' here in the cold listenin' to you two play the cute quirky couple," Darnell says and spits blood to the snow underfoot. "Enough with this philosophical cluster fuck. Get on with it already."

It's the first time I've gotten a good look at him. He stands only a few inches taller than me and he's thin and angular, with hair mowed into his scalp and features like a scarecrow. His teeth have a brown tinge to them, probably from chewing tobacco, and he wears greased stained mechanic's pants and a black hooded coat that looks like it was pulled from a dumpster, complete with cigarette burns dressing the front. When he talks, he does so with a drawl. But not like Analise's southern dialect. It's more like one of those local bumpkin slow drones as the words crawl from the back of the throat, fracturing the more heavily stressed vowels while weakening the lesser ones, making it sound like the words can't find their exit and I think, *An honest-to-God peckerwood.*

Yusuf remains quiet. He stands still, looking at his wrists which have been bound with torn bedsheets—same as Darnell. I have to hand it to both of them, neither is begging for their lives. I respect that kind of madness in a person. It seems we all have a little of it in us and, if it weren't for our current predicament, I could see us all becoming good friends on that basis alone. I may already feel a bond forming and I could get comfortable with the idea of us sharing beers over talk of art, literature, and women.

"I figured we'd just shoot them," Analise says.

"Probably better to cut their throats. Shotgun is too loud, might draw attention."

"It's hunting season."

"It's rifle season," I say, correcting her, "and there's a discernable difference in their sound. The hicks around here will know that. Someone might call it in."

"Good call. Knife it is."

"You think it's sharp enough?" I say, running my finger over the blade.

I look at Analise and the snow collecting on the fur-lined collar of her winter coat, her hair. She stares deeply, smirks, and blinks away the flakes from her eyelashes.

A perfect vision.

"What's the difference," she says and shrugs her shoulders.

"The difference is whether you're going to feel it or not."

She cocks her head slightly to the side, a hint of confusion replacing her smile and I make my move.

I throw my shoulder into hers, knocking her backward. Analise stumbles, dropping the shotgun as she tries to regain her footing. She loses and goes down hard, landing flat on her ass. She looks up at me with shock etched deep into her face, as if I've betrayed her.

But maybe I have.

I go for the gun, which has landed on the ground between us, and I swing it around to meet Darnell and Yusuf who've already started to attempt an escape, gnawing at the bedsheets with their teeth, trying to undo the knots.

"I wouldn't do that." I cock the gun.[isnt it already cocked/racked?] "I don't know what's going on and I'm not sure I give a shit. I just wanna do the job I was hired to do and get as far away from this place as I can, but you fuckin' fuckers are making that nearly impossible."

I loosen my grip on the gun and lower my aim. "Shit," I say, aiming my words at the treetops.

Darnell laughs. "Seems you're in a pickle."

I take a step forward, raise the gun, and say, "Shut up." I bite my lower lip and ease off the trigger. He's right though. I haven't thought this through. My head is fuzzy with panic. I pace the distance between Analise and the other two.

"There's no way out of this for any of us. Except maybe by finishing what was started. So go ahead and shoot us down like sick dogs."

"I would never put a dog down like this," I say, coming to a stop and looking at Darnell.

"Oh, look at you, Mr. Morality. Funny thing to say when you have the busy end of a gun pointed at the faces of two people," Darnell says.

"You started this."

"What is this, fuckin' kindergarten? Doesn't matter who started it, we're all in it now."

I glance over my shoulder at Analise, who's still on the ground, the same look of shock on her face. She's waiting for me to make a decision.

This is how I survive.

I say it, but what does it mean?

I bring my attention back to Darnell and Yusuf. I line up my shot; hear a scrambling behind me and the crunching of snow underfoot before I'm met with the feeling of something sliding into my neck and I'm instantly disarmed. I jerk back and meet Analise's gaze, reach up and pull a syringe from my neck, its plunger fully depressed. I laugh before slumping to my knees in front of her. I want to kiss her feet, but all I can do is welcome the black as my eyes flutter shut.

I wake to the feeling of a boot on my ribs, a figure hovering above me. He comes into focus. The area around his lips is badly scarred. No doubt from various squabbles with an untamed crack pipe. Deep grooves pepper his cheeks. It's a face that says, I *am who I am for what happened to me as a child.* A face that looks as though it has never felt rain.

My father is right. This man has never known the love of a good woman.

Poor bastard.

At my side lies a metal bowl, like a dog bowl. It's filled with water, maybe. Maybe some blood. On the other side of me is a scalpel, possibly a knife. I can't be sure, but I can feel nearly every part of myself as if they are separate from one another.

We're in my room. I know because I can see the bag under the bed from where I lay on the floor. Darnell, Yusuf, and Analise carry on with one another as Napoleon clucks softly from somewhere nearby, though I'm not exactly sure where. I wanna move, but the wrong direction and my skin feels like it might split down the center of my back. I feel the boot ease off my ribs and my vision blurs again as if someone has placed a dirty window between me and the rest of the world. I reach down to touch where the pain is coming from, and I feel what could be stitching running along my side.

"I wouldn't do that if I were you. For your own comfort, that is." The words come from the figure standing above me.

I don't listen.

My fingertips are enough to send pain like shrapnel through my entire body. I jerk and then seize up from the shock of it all and groan out, my throat feeling like sandpaper.

"He awake?" I hear Analise say, her voice sounding concerned. Whether it's a genuine concern or not, I can't tell. Could I ever?

"That seems to be the case. You were starting to worry that one, Fenton." He throws his head in the direction Analise's voice is coming from. "You've been out for some time now. If I had it my way, you'd be fuckin' dead, causing all this trouble, but Analise convinced me otherwise. She's taken a liking to you and has a way with words when something important to her is on the line. But a word of advice, keep a close eye on this one because pussy isn't the only thing she keeps in those panties of hers. But I suppose you already know that seeing as you got a neck full of propofol." The man laughs, a guttural laugh.

"You hush," Analise says, her voice sounding drawn out due to me being drugged.

The man squats beside me and leans in closer and I recognize him, even through fogged eyes. It's the dime store preacher from outside the diner. I knew he was a bullshit artist.

"We haven't officially met. I'm Harlan."

I laugh and then cough, the carpet beneath my shirtless torso suddenly feeling like gravel against my skin.

"Now what could a man in your position find so funny?" He asks.

I try to talk, but my sandpaper throat won't allow it. It's just as well. What I have to say will only further worsen my situation.

Analise brings me water. She lifts my head to meet the rim of a paper cup. After a few sips, she lays my head back down and I watch her feet pace the carpet alongside Darnell and Yusuf.

"Where the fuck are they?" Yusuf asks, a slight tremble in his voice.

"They'll be here," Harlan says, standing up and joining the other three on the other side of the room. "In fact, let's get everything ready to go for when they do get here. Make this transaction as quick as possible. This shit has been dragged out long enough. Darnell, grab the bag."

Darnell slides the bag out from under the bed and throws it on the mattress. I watch, my head feeling as heavy as a bowling ball. It takes every bit of strength just to lift it from the floor enough to see what's happening.

Yusuf opens the bag, removes a sleek silver box with a combination lock on it, and says, "Well ain't that fancy." He places it on the bedside table. It has a hinged door that opens from the top and looks to be made of titanium.

"Would you expect anything less from this guy?" Darnell says. "Fuckin' wop prick." He dumps a bucket of ice into the titanium box and Harlan calls for Analise to bring the goods.

"Hey, it's this *wop prick* and others like him that allow us to live better than most," Harlan says.

Analise gleefully skips into my periphery, her cupped hands full of wadded gauze that is soaked through with blood.

"Can you not skip around with that, please? The last thing we need is it rolling across this nasty fuckin' carpet," Harlan says, arms folded across his chest, his back leaning against the door. It's the first time I'm noticing he's still dressed in his priest attire.

"Oh my god," Analise says, her eyebrows forming an arch, her mouth contorting into a smile like she's about to burst out laughing. "Could you imagine that scene? Them walking in and us picking lint and blowing cigarette ash from it."

Darnell and Yusuf shake their heads.

"I think that would be the end of this gig if that were to happen," Harlan says.

At the bedside table, Analise stands at an angle, giving me a clear view from the floor as she unravels the gauze, revealing a fleshy mass that is roughly the size of my fist and shaped like a large kidney bean.

She places it in the ice-filled box, letting the gauze fall to the floor, and closes the lid.

I run my fingers along the sutures again, this time bracing myself for the pain that may follow —like a bad tooth I can't stop playing with it—and I'm reminded of crudely drawn train tracks like the ones Naomi used to draw. The ones Maddie and I hung on the refrigerator.

And there it is again. The sick sad feeling that stirs itself awake and slides through me like ground glass anytime I'm reminded of the past. It's as real and as powerful as anything else inside of me that it might as well be just another organ for them to harvest.

I wish it was.

I crawl back inside my head as everything around me dims and fades to black again.

CHAPTER: 13

Dear Maddie,

Sometimes when I'm alone I close my eyes and pretend the world has ended, because that's what it feels like anyway and since you've been gone I'm alone a lot so it might as well be true. It's been...I don't even know how long. Might as well be forever. Might as well be since yesterday. What is written in my skin seems lost on me now. I can't tell where one laceration ends, and the others begin. I used to think there was something poetic about dying and that the saddest part was that I wasn't. Now that you're gone I know this to be false. There is no uniqueness to it. It's just nothing, followed by a storm of wanting, and blame, and confusion, and when you die it's like everyone else dies too so this is only of concern to the living...

XXX

I wake, from a fever dream about Maddie, to a floating carousel of voices. They are further than before yet still closer than my own. I can feel my blood lying stagnant in my veins, thick as molasses, and every time I blink it's as if someone is scooping out the lining behind my eyes. I can sense the air moving—I watch it stir the corner of the duvet that hangs from the bed—and it feels like cheesecloth raking my skin. My chest is heavy with the weight of the past, my history having a nasty habit of moving forward to find me again and again.

Analise brings more water, wets my lips while on her knees. She smiles the kind of smile a mother would give their sick child—apologizing with her eyes, which are heavy with pity and regret, but I cannot tell if it's me or herself that she feels bad for. She wipes cold sweat from my forehead with a rag—runs her fingers through my hair.

"You're talking to her," she says and runs a damp finger along my lips, one last time.

"I never stopped." I recognize my voice but can't feel myself saying the words.

Headlights through the curtains throw vague shadows along the walls. The sound of an engine going cold and then the opening and slamming shut of car doors. More voices—Jimmy and Sal. Even from inside, I can hear their bickering about which pizza joint has a better slice—Nunzio's or Genos. Always the stereotypes.

"This is it," Harlan says, peeking through a slip in the curtain. He turns to face everyone and runs the palms of his hands down the front of his robe, smoothing out any wrinkles that may have formed. "No one say anything, I'll do the talking."

"We know. This ain't our first rodeo," Darnell says and from the tone of his voice it's evident that Darnell is sick of hearing Harlan tell everyone to keep quiet while he plays ringleader. It won't be long before Harlan has a blade in his throat, and his body dumped into a ditch.

I cough and clear my throat, doing my best to try and swallow. Analise leaves my side and takes a seat on the bed.

I push off from the floor and hold myself up on my elbows—the burn in my side feeling like a heavyweight boxer throwing jabs from the inside out. I wanna puke, but I hold it down and wait, and my head feels like a bug-zapper sounds.

Feels like an eternity.

I think of the family that now resides in my home. After Maddie died and the bank foreclosed on our house, it was sold to a young couple with three children. I went back once and parked across the street. I sat there for hours and watched the young wife tend to the garden—the one that Maddie built—and criticized her the entire time because that's not how Maddie would have done it. She loved that garden, and she was amazing with plants and now this young dumb white thing was fucking it all up. I watched the children come home from school and run around in the yard and after their father came home, I watched the kids skip inside happily after being called for dinner. I hated them for no reason other than jealousy. They had what I wanted and let slip through my fingers.

After the sun went down and the lights started going off, I thought about sneaking in through the basement window—I'd wondered if the man of the house knew about the broken latch—and murdering all five of them in their sleep, after which I would scrawl the words SHE NEVER LEFT on the walls in their blood for dramatic effect. Nowadays I mostly think about going in when everyone's gone and killing myself on their nice expensive furniture.

The knock comes and before I let it register, I'm yelling, "They gotta gun aimed at the door."

It's amazing how a simple lie can bring everything crashing down.

It's amazing how the truth can do the same thing.

My voice is weak, but it's loud enough because there's no hesitation on Jimmy and Sal's part. A bullet rips through the door and tears into Darnell's cheekbone, blowing out the other side of his face and sending his teeth skipping across the carpet like some fucked up game of back-alley dice.

Whoever rolled that hand, lost.

Darnell goes down, bleeding terribly, but not dead yet. He'll have time to think about where it all went wrong and, at this moment, I almost feel bad for him.

The gunshot sends everyone into panic mode. Analise drops to the carpet on her stomach to avoid any further gunfire. Harlan produces a .32 pistol he had tucked into a well-hidden holster underneath his robe and crams himself in the corner, just left of the door, waiting to take out anyone who enters. Napoleon caws, flaps his wings and glides from somewhere above, coming to rest on the floor before hunkering himself under the bed for protection.

The poor bird survived cockfights only to end up having to deal with this shit.

Yusuf retrieves the shotgun leaning against the dresser and takes a stance next to me. He fires off a round, taking out the glass of the bay window and, in the sudden excitement, I grab the scalpel from the carpet next to me and jam it through Yusuf's foot, pinning him to the floor. He screams out in agonizing pain as more bullets come through the door, walls, and window, taking out lamps, picture frames, and chunks of the headboard. I watch the telephone on the bedside table explode into pieces and the pillows get torn to rags, their stuffing now floating through the room that's been transformed into a gun range.

Still screaming, Yusuf throws a jab in a downward motion with the butt of the shotgun—in an attempt to cave in my skull—but I roll away, and staying low, crab crawl backward into the bathroom, and slam the door shut with my foot. Leaning against the toilet, I suck back air as sweat pours in rivers, and I can feel how pale I am. The burn in my side is growing. It feels like I'm about to give birth through the incision.

Gunfire continues to roll around in the next room. I can hear Jimmy, Sal, Yusuf, and Harlan exchanging colorful language between shots— insults about each other's backgrounds and upbringings—stray bullets now coming through the wall and door of the bathroom. I scramble for the tub, pull myself up by the lip, and throw myself inside.

I take a few deep breaths, bracing myself before I make my next move.

Squatting in the tub, I grab hold of its edge, the one at my back, and lifting myself up, I throw my feet out to kick the toilet tank, immediately dropping back down inside to shield myself as more shots come through the walls and pulverizes the sheetrock which is dusting down my head and chest.

It's an echo chamber in here. I hold my hands over my ears and wait for the buzzing to stop. When

I think it's safe, I repeat the process, my side burning with every failed attempt.

"For fuck's sake!"

Everything in this place is held together with duct tape and super glue, but not this toilet. This thing is rooted in the fucking earth.

"C'mon!"

One more try and my feet break clean through the toilet tank, spilling water, along with the gun, to the floor. I lie back down and wait, but nothing comes. No gunfire, no voices.

I lift myself out once more, balancing myself at the waist on the lip of the tub. I reach for the Ziploc bag containing the revolver, stretching myself as far as I can. The sutures give way. I can feel blood slide from my body in great leaky gulps.

Gun in hand, I drop back down into the cast iron tub as what remains of the door is thrown open with a muscled shoulder.

It's Yusuf. He's looking as bad as I feel. He peers down at the mess of porcelain and water at his feet. He peeks into the tub, sees me curled up inside with the gun aimed directly at his face. He lifts his shotgun and I quickly fire off a round, catching him in the neck, sending red spray along the wall and busted mirror. He clutches at the hole and coughs up blood, a look of confusion on his face, before slumping to his knees and catching his head on the corner of the sink as he falls to the floor.

Six bullet chamber, four bullets remain.

Above me, a pair of Analise's panties hang from the towel rack which is fixed to the wall and still intact. I pull them from the chrome ringlet, wad them up, and jam the flower-patterned underwear into the mouth of the wound at my side to keep from any further blood loss.

Like it matters.

I feel nearly weightless at this point— like I could just float up and out of the tub, through the motel roof, and into the night sky to kiss the stars clean.

I remove myself from the tub and maneuver around Yusuf's dead body. I wipe busted sheetrock from my face and neck. Bending over, I pull the still embedded scalpel from Yusef's foot and slip it in my back pocket, then I use the wall to balance myself, leaving streaks of blood trailing along the wallpaper as I move. The panties stuffed into my side are doing very little. They are already a wad of sticky red, the weight of them from all the blood they've absorbed causing it to slip out of the wound and hang in the open air, like a gas-soaked rag unfurling itself from a Molotov cocktail.

Keeping the gun aimed, low but ready, I peek around the door fixture and the first thing I see is Sal framed by the broken window. He's slumped over the sill, half his body falling into the motel room, his lower half exposed to the cold outside. Behind him a strong wind blows, pushing snow past his limp form and into the room, coating everything in white. From where I am, it looks like Sal has taken a gut shot and from the sound of it, he's still alive. I hear him frantically gasping for air, doing his best to hold onto life.

I eye the corners of the room in search of Harlan, but I don't see him anywhere. I step further into the room and am immediately met with the cold coming in through the busted window. I swear I see steam coming from the incision and it's the first time I'm realizing that I have no shoes on, the carpet damp beneath my feet.

The place is destroyed, as one would expect after a place is lit up with gunfire. All of the lamps in the room, as well as the ceiling light, have been shot out, and the space is now dimly lit by only the neon sign out front. In the scuffle of everyone dodging bullets, the nightstand has been tipped over. The titanium box lies on its side and my kidney has been dumped onto the motel carpet. It rests in front of the door near Darnell's lifeless body. I watch Napoleon peck at it, first with curiosity, then like he hasn't eaten in weeks. I laugh, because somehow it makes sense. I shoo Napoleon away with my foot. He flaps his wings at me and scuttles off into a corner. I look down at my kidney. Poke at it with the tip of my toes.

How am I still alive? Why am I still alive?

I squat down, and, clutching at my side to keep Analise's panties firmly planted inside my open wound, I pick my kidney up off the floor. How long does it take meat to spoil? How long was I out? Which of these mooks has the knowledge to perform something as delicate as removing an organ? I was wrong about them; they're not just some backwoods bumpkins.

I slink closer to the window and can hear Sal trying to talk through the liquid that is collecting in his throat. It's all gargles and bloody spit dripping from his mouth. It hangs in thick strands from his lips. He looks pitiful. I have no choice but to put a bullet in his head, if for no other reason than I don't want to listen to him choke on his own fluids. I put the gun to the back of his skull.

"Fuck you, Sal. I never did like you, you fuckin' Guinea prick."

I pull the trigger—decorate the thin layer of snow at my feet with bits of skull fragments, brain matter, and blood, and I am filled with a satisfaction that seems to come with ending the life of someone you've always despised, no matter how trivial the reason.

Or maybe it's just me. Maybe this shit gets easier the more you do it. Either way, it's what I imagine I'd feel like if I were to kill myself. But of course, I could never revel in that, so I suppose this is the next best thing.

After all, beggars can't be choosers.

I look out through the broken window and see Jimmy's body sprawled across the parking lot; a pool of blood already having formed around his body and trailing toward the motel door. Far as I can figure it, he tried taking cover behind the car but was taken out before he got there and bled to death where he lays now. I think about firing off a round into his already bullet-ridden torso just for the hell of it, but I leave that urge to sit inside me, planning to aim it elsewhere.

I take one last look at my kidney which I still hold tightly in my fist. Blood squeezes itself through my clenched fingers. I wanna blow it to pieces with the remaining bullets that are tucked into the chamber of the revolver, but instead, I just think *Fuck it, there's no use in wasting the bullets,* and toss it through the shattered window and into the cold dark outside, where it rolls through the snow and escapes from my sight.

In the time it takes me to turn around and walk back toward the bathroom, Harlan has crept from the closet and has me on the floor, knocking the gun from my hand. It lands with a thud and discharges, wasting a bullet on the leg of the dresser that holds the TV. I scramble for it, but he reaches the mark before I do. He pulls me up to my knees by a handful of my hair and presses the barrel into my cheek.

Why didn't I think to check there and what the fuck is it with people hiding in closets waiting to take me out?

I let out a lazy laugh—the only kind of laugh that bleeding out allows—and say, "I knew you were a scumbag, but I didn't take you for this kind of scumbag."

"Yeah, what kind would that be?" He presses the gun harder into my cheek. I feel the barrel against my cheekbone making it hard to answer, but I talk through the minor inconvenience, forming my words around the blood in my mouth.

"The kind that kills a man with his own gun."

"Well, sorry to be a disappointment." He cocks the trigger.

Six bullet chamber, two bullets remain.

"Now open your mouth." He barks the words.

I don't do what he says.

"I said open your fucking mouth." And before he even gives me that second chance, he's pushing the barrel into my mouth. I can hear the scrape of steel against my teeth.

Everything is louder from the inside of the skull.

He leans into the gun, forcing it further in and eventually down my throat. I gag and cough, stomach acid, blood, and vomit forcing itself up around the barrel. It drips down my chin and to the carpet below us.

Harlan lets out a guttural laugh. "You look like one of them whores getting a rough face fuck in some porno movie."

And then, I watch Analise crawl out from under the bed on her stomach. She gracefully and quietly lifts herself up off the floor and onto her feet. She says Harlan's name in a near whisper, but it is all I need because it throws his attention off just long enough for me to regain the upper hand.

I search myself for one last surge of energy and I find it in the contempt I have for myself. I think of Maddie, Naomi, and my parents—even my sister— and I think of all the wrongs I've done that lead to this miserable as fuck situation. In turn, I think about the consequences they'll have to bear because of it. I think about all of this, and I lunge at Harlan. We go back, landing on the bed, where I pin him under my weight. I wrestle the gun free from his hand and put a bullet up under his ribcage. His face contorts into a look of horrendous pain—a pain I don't have to imagine. I slip the scalpel from my back pocket and lay into him, screaming. I can hear the tearing of flesh and the crunching of cartilage as I stab at his neck, head, and face in quick successive jabs—one after the other, again and again—finally leaving the scalpel embedded in the corner of his eye.

CHAPTER: 14

Analise and I kneel on the bed next to Harlan's body, facing one another. I lean into her shoulder to hold myself up. She wipes the blood away from under my eyes with her thumbs. I play with the frayed fabric at the hem of her dress.

She tells me that she's part of a roving collective of organ harvesters—along with Harlan, Yusuf, and Darnell. She says they call themselves the NETAHEY, which she claims is an Apache term for "Avowed Killers." They work solely for the rich, those who are in need of organs, but whose money doesn't matter to the world of medicine and insurance companies. Harlan was the brains; working under the guise of a preacher to either sniff out potential donors or recruit new people to aid him in what he hoped would be a lucrative future.

Corsetti.

His son.

It was all a setup, right from the very beginning. All to save his child, and I can't even blame him.

"What about the guy in the closet?" I ask, my voice weak and starting to fade.

"That was just a coincidence."

"Whose place was I at then?"

"He never told us. He had the bag planted there to look more convincing. The guy in the closet was just a hiccup."

"That's why the body was never found," I say.

She nods. "He sent Darnell and Harlan over to clean up the scene and dispose of the body to not further complicate things," she laughs. "Like that mattered."

Some things just don't add up though. It all seems a bit theatrical. He could have just as easily called me into his office or sent Jimmy and Sal to knock me over the head. I don't know if I believe her entirely, but I don't believe she planned to fall in love with me either.

"There's something else," she says.

"It gets better?" I let out a tired laugh as a tremor works its way up my spine and into my skull.

"Harlan wanted to kill you after the operation, but I convinced him we could use you as a mule. It was to buy you more time." She strokes my hair, kisses the top of my head. "Buy *us* more time."

"A mule? In what way?"

"There's a bag of heroin in place of your kidney. 100% pure. A man can hold more drugs than a rooster."

I try to angle my head to give myself a better view of the room and to look for the bird but my face remains planted in Analise's shoulder. "So that's the truth about Napoleon."

"Everything I told you was the truth. I just left that bit out."

"You said, "Buy *us* more time." More time for what?" I ask, the words riding my fading breath.

"To formulate a plan. A way out of all this. Together."

Analise says "together," and I can hear the longing in her voice. A woman who's desperate for love and attention, but this could never work. Not now. All trust has been broken on both ends. I mean, we've already made attempts on each other's lives.

It's starting to become a real relationship.

"So, there's a bag of heroin inside me right now?"

Analise nods. "There is. If you reach inside and feel around for it, you'll find it."

And like everything else, I have no choice but to take her word for it because I don't have it in me to fist fuck my own wound in search of possible drugs. The pain and loss of blood have caught up with me. I've survived everything up to this point, but I won't survive this. Nor do I want to.

"What the fuck am I supposed to do with this?"

"The heroin?"

"No, this information."

"I'm just trying to be honest."

"Well, you picked a pretty piss poor time to come clean. It does nothing for me now. Look at me, I'm a fucking bloody dishrag of a human being."

"I'm sorry," she says, and this time I hear sincerity in her voice. I cock my head slightly, angling my head on her shoulder to look up at her. She's crying, streaks of black running down her face and I realize for the first time that few things are as beautiful as runny mascara on a woman whose heart is aching for something I will never understand.

I push away from her and hold myself up to meet her eye to eye. We lean into one another, and our lips meet.

Our first kiss.

Our tongues dance—her mouth wetter than anything that came before it.

It tastes exactly how I thought it would.

She pulls my head away from hers, spits in my mouth, rakes the corner of her bottom lip with her teeth—murders me with her eyes. And then we're back at it again. I wanna tell her how I wish things could have worked out between us, about Naomi, and about the time when I was seven and was awakened one night by the sound of something in the wall behind my bed. About how the anxiety of not knowing what was there or what the outcome would be if I were to find out is a feeling I still carry with me, but instead I reach out to pull the scalpel from Harlan's face and stick her in the neck, puncturing her carotid and killing her almost instantly. She goes limp against my frame and I whisper in her ear, hoping she hears me before the flame is completely snuffed out.

"You are not her. You never could be."

I let her fall to the bed next to Harlan. I search their bodies for cigarettes and when I come up empty I search Yusuf and Darnell, finding a soft pack tucked into Darnell's pants pocket. I fire one up and sit, slumped over, on the edge of the bed and I hear Maddie clearer than I ever have since she died.

"If you love, you lose, that is the rule."

I think about leaving a note explaining everything. But how do you explain a scene like this? And then I laugh, between drags of the cigarette, thinking of the local law enforcement trying to figure this one out. Five scumbags, a raving beauty, and one half-stitched-up asshole missing a kidney lying dead in a room. A drug deal gone horribly wrong, perhaps? Were they all fighting over the same woman? Was it bad sex between all of them? Maybe they all took turns fucking this guy's wound? How does the bird play a role in all of this and did this sick fuck feed pieces of his own kidney to it before tossing it out the window? I think of all this and smile at the thought of the work they have ahead of them.

I choke on the cigarette, spit blood to the floor, and feel something slide deep within me. A voice, maybe, but not Maddie's or anyone else I know. It's more a voice of reason—a different kind of dying. Not the kind you fight to push away from but the kind you welcome. And I do welcome it.

Corsetti is going to have a fit once he finds out what's happened here. Once he realizes his son is just as dead as the rest of us. He'll want some sort of retribution and he'll look to Naomi and possibly to the rest of my family, but not if I'm dead. He's not that kind of guy. There will be no point because there will be no one to enact revenge against, no one to teach a lesson to.

Six bullet chamber, one bullet remains.

I take the revolver from the mattress, where it's fallen between Harlan's legs, and lazily twirl it around my finger. I remove the bullet from the cylinder and wet the tip with my tongue. I roll it around in my fist—breathe Maddie's name into my closed palm before sliding the bullet back into position. I spin the cylinder one final time and think of my father. I slap it shut on my knee.

If you love, you lose, that is the rule and without exception. Sometimes to other people, sometimes to death. Other times to dreams you couldn't possibly play a role in, or because of your own wrongdoing.

Your gardens will rot, your children will die, you'll bury your dog and watch the ones you care about walk away and never look back. We all know it, yet it doesn't stop us from reaching out from the edges of our own madness just to grab that little bit of good—something, anything that'll make it all just a bit more bearable, ignoring the fact that we're setting ourselves up for the worst kind of pain. It is inevitable and it is profoundly unfair. And you'll try to make sense of the pain that is left in its wake, but you'll fail. It's just simply the way it has to be because life is like that sometimes.

I flick my cigarette against the wall and watch ash and embers ride an updraft of wind blowing in through the window. I look down at my shirtless self, at my body like a prison cell wall. The inmates tracking the days they've been incarcerated. I guess we all do time in some form or another. Some of us in large buildings made of cement and steel, others inside our own heads.

I breathe deep, feel it rattle in my ribcage and the pain is as bad as it's going to get.

This is as good a grave as any I suppose.

I tilt my face toward the ceiling and corkscrew the barrel of the revolver into my mouth until it's flat against the roof. I cock the trigger and close my eyes.

Outside, the sun is coming up. Even with my eyes closed, I can feel the world getting slightly brighter. I think it's finally going to be a beautiful day.

Click...click...click...

Philip LoPresti is an author and photographer living in upstate New York. He's an avid music fan and an obsessive film fanatic. When he's not writing or photographing everything he's usually reading Cormac McCarthy novels or watching horror, crime, and western films. You can view his photography on his site **philiplopresti.com** or on his Instagram **philip_lopresti**.